Fiction
Book 2026

AN T-EILEAN DORCHA
(THE DARK ISLAND)

GORDON IAN MACLEOD

Other Novels by Gordon MacLeod

Silicon Glen

76

Just a Little Drop More

Beyond the Tree at Mamre

Carrot Toppers

Pods for Pigs

Proscription

Works for Stage, Radio & Screen

Absent Friends

44(1) (b)

Where Did All the Flowers Come From?

The Gatekeeper (unpublished)

A Haggis Sausage Roll (unpublished)

On the Breadline

Molios

A Clyde Hogmanay (unpublished)

© Copyright 2025 by Gordon MacLeod, all rights reserved.

No part of this publication may be reproduced, stored in a retrieval system, or transmitted, in any form or by any means, electronic, mechanical, photocopying, recording, or otherwise, without the written permission of the author.

http://gordonmacleod.weebly.com

Author's Note to the Reader

The events and characters in this novel are works of fiction and in no way represent real events.
Some place names may be real, however that is where all similarity ends.

CHAPTER 1 BEFORE SUNRISE
CHAPTER 2 WHAT'S THERE NOT TO LIKE?
CHAPTER 3 IT'S THE ECONOMY, STUPID
CHAPTER 4 AN ACTION GROUP
CHAPTER 5 THE RESISTANCE
CHAPTER 6 SPLITTING HAIRS
CHAPTER 7 ART AND DESIGN
CHAPTER 8 ROAST
CHAPTER 9 SACCHARIN SWEETENERS
CHAPTER 10 THE GRAVY TRAIN
CHAPTER 11 TWITCHERS
CHAPTER 12 TWIT TWOO
CHAPTER 13 ROTARY BLADES
CHAPTER 14 BREAKING WIND
CHAPTER 15 A CROWDED BAR
CHAPTER 16 TIMBER
CHAPTER 17 D-DAY

CHAPTER 18 SAILING CLOSE TO THE WIND

CHAPTER 19 REASSEMBLING

CHAPTER 20 CRUCIFIXION

CHAPTER 21 THE FALL OUT

CHAPTER 22 BRIA WOODS

POSTFACE

BEFORE SUNRISE

These are the woods at Glen Bria, shortly before sunrise, on a cool and relatively clear morning in the late winter.

Although they lie a little inland, and form part of what was once an ancient forest, the hypnotic sound of running water from a nearby river can be heard, tirelessly running down the sloping land adjacent to a track which is partially illuminated by moonlight through the trees, and which runs through the length of the woods.

Old wooden posts which are clad in ivy, give an unkempt appearance of wise old men badly in need of haircuts, and who watch from the sidelines, as the first few dog walkers, trying to beat the dog-walking rush hour appear.

As they survey the partially lit path, they are unsure whether or not the twilight demands the need for the light of their torches.
It's certainly dark under the cover of branches which neither moonlight nor sunlight has penetrated through, as yet.
Some opt for it, others against, as crows unseen laugh, either in derision, or, at their indecision.
The horses in the nearby field, despite their *neighing,* are in fact only passing comment on the disturbance the people and their dogs are causing.

The eastern sky starts to emit a red hue, and is glimpsed through the opening to a field in which the horses are framed, heralding the arrival of the Sun and daybreak.

Very slowly it begins to emerge, easing itself up from its celestial bed which lies below the horizon. As the earth rotates, shafts of light start to lighten up the stage below, between the trunks and skeletal branches of trees which have had their leaves shorn during the last gale, and upon which squirrels from the heights above, throw nuts and acorns at the dog walkers, and now the joggers who pass by below.

As a man approaches a body of water, on the opposite side of the track close to where the river flows, isolated on its own lies the remnant of what was once a much larger lochan.

As he proceeds on his walk, slightly further north, he comes across another body of water, which is nothing more than a large puddle.

Situated right beside the puddle, is a very large electricity pylon.

A squirrel looks up and appears startled by the intrusion, as its tail stops wagging vigorously doing brushstrokes in the air, having retrieved its acorn from a previous season's burial.

The path which he is taking, once formed an old cart track, and is no longer really used to take people and their luggage between the villages on their journeys, or, to carry the mail, though it is still used by horses as a bridleway, and some people still do cycle on it to reach their respective destinations.

But there is no need to be watching out for highwaymen.

The only lookout is a buzzard, perched on one of the spider-like arms and legs that form the naked branches of a tree.

Either he has fled the nest, in response to the discordant *twee* of his young, or he is already up and out hunting, canvassing with interest the landscape for prey.

He's certainly dis-interested in the two schoolboys who appear on their bicycles, and who stop by the six monolithic stones, which on closer inspection can be found to be adorned with cup and ring motifs. The stones lie a few yards off the track, and serve as an access point to a field, but instead this morning, they serve as a rendezvous point, at which to smoke some cannabis, and like squirrels, bury the remainder somewhere close by, for retrieval and later use.

Having entered the track by the Shee Gate, where peace and tranquility reign, as they approach the Clachan Gate to the north, beyond which the neighbouring village lies, the surroundings change. Beyond that gate, there is a modern plantation of Sitka spruce and pine, and the distant rumble of traffic can be heard on the nearby coastal road.

It is about a forty minute walk between the two localities along the track. In ancient times, there was probably only one settlement, as the next thing you come across are the remains of old round houses, which are hardly discernible to the untrained eye, except for a few mounds of stone which lie underfoot, barely breaking the surface of the soil, if at all.

Under an old road bridge as you approach the village beyond the Clachan Gate, graffiti can be seen to cover the underside of the bridge and its supporting walls, complete with gangland type jargon and sexually explicit phraseology. There is much beyond the Clachan Gate that is less than desirable, and which seeks to contaminate all that lies within Glen Bria, and beyond.

WHAT'S THERE NOT TO LIKE?

As he awoke the next morning to a light drumroll on his window pane, he got up from his bed, looked out of the window, and simply remarked,
'I don't like this'.

His wife, Jean, turned round, and through half closed eyes muttered,
'What's there not to like about it?'

But it was too late, he was gone.
In a matter of minutes he had dressed, brushed his teeth, or at least those that remained, and having put on his long overcoat, was walking headlong into the breeze and up the Bria Main Road.

'I don't like this', he remarked by way of opening to the shopkeeper.

'It's not the nicest', Mike consoled.

'It's the kind of drizzle that soaks you right through to the bone', exaggerated John, wiping down the sheen that had settled on his overcoat.

'Is it the paper you're after?' asked Mike, holding his Courier aloft.

'Yes, thanks… and six ounces of fudge please', interjected John quickly, in case he forgot his one illicit pleasure in life.

'I think you are one of the few shoppers who are left, who come in here and ask for fudge in ounces', informed Mike.

'And long may you still be here selling it', said John with pleading in his eyes.

'I've no plans to be going anywhere', Mike comforted. 'Fifty three years this month it has been in the family, and if I get my way, it'll *still* be in the family, in another fifty three'.

'Good on you', exclaimed John in satisfaction at the emphatic response, as this was his favourite shop.
In fact, it was now the only shop in the village, where you could buy anything.

As he walked home with the wind behind his back, he reminisced about how five years ago, the only bank left in the village had closed.
To think there used to be two here, he thought.

'You can always do your banking at the Post Office', they had stated emphatically at a public meeting in response to the villagers' objections, but despite the promises, that closed soon after, only to be replaced by a Post Office van that visited twice a week from the mainland.
But even that was not guaranteed, nor a service, as often it could not get an internet signal to enable it to process transactions.

Yes, much had changed on the Dark Isle.
The latest to go was the Doctor's surgery following the pandemic, and now you had to travel the three miles to Clachan to find one. That was of course, if you were lucky to get an appointment in the phone lottery that opened at 8.30a.m. each weekday morning.

That journey might have been easier several years ago too, had they not cut the bus service to twice a day during the school year, and to once a day, if it was at any other time of year.

Rather than go home by the route which he had come, he made a detour off into the woods.

And that is why this is so important, he concluded, as he entered the track enclosed by the overhanging trees.

Taking out the paper packet with the fudge from his pocket, he put some in his mouth, taking time to savour the taste of vanilla and its texture.
In the back of his mind, he could hear the voice of his wife, as if she was there present, saying aloud,
'That stuff will be the death of you'.

He smiled in acknowledgment and walked on.

A mile further away, standing on the old road bridge and looking down onto the track, stood Brian Whittington.
Turning to his chief surveyor, he smiled a satisfied smile to himself, and simply said, 'What's there not to like about it?'

Reaching his home, by the path that led into the heart of the village, John removed the newspaper from under his overcoat and unrolled it on the kitchen counter top.

'Would you like a cup of tea, dear?' his wife, Jean, offered.

'Yes, thank you', her husband responded, returning from having hung his slightly damp overcoat on the peg in the hallway.

'It's not the nicest', John suggested, for the most part being a man of little words and simply regurgitating his opening to the shopkeeper.

Jean simply nodded, knowing that the weather was but another excuse for giving expression to his pessimism.

'It's the kind of drizzle that soaks you right through to the bone', John offered by way of commentary.

'Oh', said Jean, having heard this opening gambit countless times before.
As John ruffled through the paper, he looked up and round the side of it at his wife.

'Anything of interest?' she asked.

'Nothing ever happens here', he retorted and returned behind the drab world of newspaper print.

There was a pause.

'Good God!' came the most unusual of expressions from behind the paper, for John was not known to make such remarks, being a God-fearing man.

Jean looked startled. The last time she could recall him having become so animated, was when the eldest of their two daughters, Sheila, announced on a visit that she was getting a divorce.

'What is it? What have you found?' she asked with a sense of excitement in her voice.

'Here, hidden away in all the planning applications…', John informed.

Who reads the planning applications in a newspaper, thought Jean.

'…is a notice to build a Windfarm of six turbines, extending from the east side of Glen Bria, right through the heart of the woods'.

'But they can't', Jean suggested, doubting the information.

'They can you know. Look, it says so here', he advised, opening the paper wide for her to see.

Sure enough, as she fumbled on the table for her reading glasses, finding them there and putting them on, she read the same planning notice he had referred to.

The proposed turbines, each with a height of 160 metres, were to generate enough energy to supply the island.

'But they can't, she restated more emphatically this time than before.

'Yes, they can', said John just as emphatically.

'Too many people will object', Jean asserted, 'and what about the Environment Protection Agency?'

'What about them?' John countered, 'they're nothing but a useless quango'.

'That's not true, John', said Jean, doubting the veracity of her own statement.

'Look at the state of the water?' smirked John.

'It doesn't give much hope for faith', he suggested, before quickly adding, 'in public agencies', should he have misspoken heretically.

'But what about the people, love?' proposed Jean. 'They can't just ignore their objections'.

'What objections?' asked John in a derisory tone. 'Will anyone even care enough to object?' he asked rhetorically.

'Of course, they will, love', Jean consoled. 'You can't just ignore a strong local voice. That would be electoral suicide'.

'Aye, but you forget we only have one Councillor for the island. The other councillors outnumber him'.

'Who are they?' she asked slightly bemused.

'They're all from the mainland...they will be the ones who will benefit financially from any proposed development', he concluded.

'How can they *benefit?*' asked Jean with disbelief in her voice.

'Look, it says, money will be provided if the development goes ahead, to improve community facilities in the Council area'.

'But that's like...bribery!' Jean exclaimed.

'Exactly', John agreed, 'Look, there is a notice of a drop-in event in the notices section'.

'When?' asked Jean.

'Next Friday, at Clachan Village Hall, from midday through to three o'clock'.

'Well, you can go and object, John, can't you?'

'I can, but I don't like this, Jean, I don't like it at all'.

IT'S THE ECONOMY, STUPID

Brian Whittington had prepared himself for the Council meeting, as he brushed down the front of his suit with his hand.

He had heard it all so many times before, that he knew what to expect.

There would be the token objections from Councillors in relation to the predicted noise the turbines might make. But as he knew fine well, the developments in technology rendered these objections obsolete. He could easily take Councillors to another development and demonstrate they make no more of an auditory impact than road traffic when heard at a distance.

Much harder to deal with were the objections on health grounds, which ranged from people suffering from poor sleep, increased stress, through to hearing loss and congenital abnormalities.
The problem was there just was no evidence to support any of these claims.

But just as hard to counter, were those who objected to proposed windfarm developments on environmental grounds.
They would cite the visual impact and the implications for wildlife.

'So, just how are we meant to respond to those claims?' asked his Chief Surveyor as they approached the door to the Council Chamber.

Brian sat there and was invited to talk to the proposed development.

His PowerPoint presentation was glitzy, his spoken words well-rehearsed and his answers well-polished. This may have been the twelfth such occasion he had been called upon to talk about such developments, across the country, for the company.

As predicted, he countered the noise argument, by inviting the Councillors on the Committee to attend a site of similar size.

The company would lay on a luxury coach for them, ensuring they were taken to the four star hotel for lunch that lay in the neighbouring village close to the site, but far enough away so that when they got out the coach before they were sumptuously wined and dined, they would hear no noise.

Cost was no object given the long-term gain the shareholders would reap.

The health arguments he encountered, were to some degree easily rebutted, by drawing attention to the lack of empirical evidence to support any such claims.

He was also able to draw the attention of Councillors to a recent protest that was ridiculed in the mainstream press, where protesters who had been citing electro-magnetic radiation from windturbines as a problem, were pictured wearing tin foil hats in a sit-down protest outside a site.

He had a picture of this on his PowerPoint presentation, which produced a hearty laugh from all, which echoed around the Chamber.

They had liked that one, he thought telling himself that he must make more use of it at future events.

Then came the Green Councillor, from a Ward in the Council area on the mainland, where a previous more modest development had taken place several years previously.

His political opponents in the Chamber, of which there were many, were quick to remind him of that fact.

He had argued with Brian, trying to get him to concede that they would have to fell some of the trees in woods at Glen Bria, to ensure the turbines would benefit from the coastal winds coming in off the sea. But Brain had rejected this.

So, the impact on wildlife was the first objection. In response, Brian had pointed out that the number of jobs that would be created would be of great benefit to the local community.

But this did not stop the Green Councillor. 'It's no more than environmental destruction', he asserted aloud.

'Rubbish', shouted an opposing Councillor. 'I thought you were about protecting the environment, by *supporting* renewable energy projects?'

The Convenor of the Committee intervened, with a direct question to Brian.

'Just how many jobs are we talking about?' he asked.

'Nationally, we are talking about 30,000 jobs across the renewables industry', suggested Brian. 'I can't be precise in terms of the local numbers, but we are talking lots of construction jobs for local people'.

'It's a no brainer', one Councillor interjected.

'But what about the impact on the wildlife?' the Green Councillor insisted, but was rudely cut off by another whose voice could be heard retorting, 'It's about the economy, stupid'.

When the local Councillor from the Dark Isle started to express concern about the visual impact of the development, and gave a cautionary warning that removing trees from the woods would be detrimental to tourism in the local area, Brian played his ace card.

'The law enables us to provide grants to promote community projects to enhance the local environment and local infrastructure in the council's area', he informed.

That brought about a momentary silence in the Chamber, interrupted by the island's Councillor.

'I hope the grants will benefit local projects on the island. I would remind the chamber that only last financial year, the Council withdrew funding to support public toilet facilities on the island'.

A few grumbles could be heard in the room.

Then Brian seized the opportunity with his pièce de resistance.

'We have a community consultation event next week in Clachan Village Hall, on Dark Island, during which we will listen to any concerns that local residents may have, as well as finding out from them any local facilities and infrastructure that need funding for future re-development'.

'But the Hall is pretty run-down', countered the island's Councillor.

'Yes, these are precisely the very type of facilities that we would hope to help refurbish and revitalize for the benefit of the whole community', Brian stressed in response, feeling rather pleased with himself that the Councillor had fallen into his trap.

The Council's Planning Committee resolved to reconvene in one month after the community consultation event had been held, to determine the outcome of the application, and following the visit the next week to a similar site to that which was being proposed. Followed by the hearty lunch, of course.

This would give the necessary time for any objections to be lodged, before a final decision was made of whether or not to approve the scheme.

AN ACTION GROUP

'Can I have a half and a half?' John asked the barman.

'I wouldn't have thought you'd be having anything else', smirked Calum.

'Did you see that in the Courier?' enquired John.

'What?' said Calum, turning back to the counter with the drinks in hand, showing his usual disinterest in anything newsworthy on the island.

'The Planning application to build six turbines up in Glen Bria and through the woods', said John emphatically.

'That'll be six pounds twenty please, John', said Calum before pausing in thought. 'They'll get plenty wind up there', he suggested.

John put the money on the counter in disgust.

'They'll get plenty from in here more like', retorted John, turning around with his two drinks in hand and he went and sat down at a table.

'What did I say?' asked Calum rhetorically, hands in the air turning to another customer sat at the bar, in a further display of mocking disinterest.

John fidgeted with the paper packet with the fudge in it which was in his pocket.
He was soon joined by his friend, Archie.

'How's it going?' asked his tall friend, a balding man of about seventy years of age, which was hidden underneath the all too familiar tweed cap which he wore, but was also built like a tank.
Despite his intimidating stature, he was what people called a gentle giant.

'Aye, fine', said John, before adding, 'well it's naw fine actually'.

'Oh, why naw?' asked Archie.

'Did you naw see in the Courier the Planning application to build six turbines up in Glen Bria and right through into the woods?' John asked.

'Naw, where was that? In the small print?' joked Archie, before adding, 'mind you, it's all bloody small print to me these days'.

'It was in the back pages under planning applications', John replied. 'There was also a meeting about it next Friday, mentioned in the Notices section'.

'I dunna read the back page, except for the sport', said Archie. 'Where's the meeting?'

'Clachan Village Hall, next Friday afternoon', informed John. 'Are you coming?'

'I suppose', said Archie, unsure of his own feelings on the matter and beginning to regret agreeing without knowing them, or, just what he might be getting into. He knew John well, and from experience could tell he was about to get intensely involved in some cause.

It was the same at work. John was not one for letting things pass. If there was a wrong to be righted, John would be right there in the heart of things. It was what made him a good Union Steward, after all. Mind you, he thought, they had all cause to be grateful for that on occasions.

'It can't go ahead', John insisted, banging his half pint glass on the table. The noise raised a few eyebrows of other people at the bar.

'Will you watch my glasses!' Calum shouted over in jest.

'You feel very strongly about this', said Archie, before adding, 'I can tell, you know'.

'Too right I feel strongly about it, Archie. It will be the death knell of this island'.

'Is that naw a bit strong, John?' remarked Archie, beginning to regret even making the suggestion. 'It's only six turbines after all'.

'Aye, but each one is *160 metres* tall, Archie!' John exclaimed. 'That's taller than the pyramid of Giza', he added.

'I've never seen it', said Archie.

'Higher than the Blackpool tower then, or the Wallace and Scott Monuments combined', snorted John. 'They will drive people out of their homes, and think about all the animals in the woods. Bria will never be the same again. Tourists aren't going to want to come to the island, and visit the Glen, with six massive stilts wi' a propeller standing on them, towering above them'.

'I suppose naw', said Archie, thoughtfully, conceding some of John's points.

Both had been quite engrossed in their conversation, so much so, they had been oblivious to their former colleague, Murdoch, who had retired a few years before them, and his wife, Rhea, approaching them from behind.

On feeling the tap on his shoulder, John turned around to face them.

'Can I get you gentlemen another drink?' Murdoch offered.

'Naw, you're fine, from me', said John, before Archie chipped in.

'None for me either, thanks', he said.

Murdoch and his wife went up to the bar, returning shortly thereafter to the table where John and Archie sat, with drinks in hand.

'What were you getting so animated about?' Murdoch enquired, also knowing how John had a tendency to get involved in all sorts of business.

'I was telling Archie about the wind farm that is being proposed for Glen Bria. Did you read about it?' John queried.

'Aye, it was in the paper this morning. I was just saying myself to Rhea, just how it'll be a scar on the landscape. But it's no so much the appearance, it's the rotating blades of the turbines on these things which cause so many of the problems', he responded.

'Exactly!' cried John.

'We've got twenty eight days from the date of publication to make objections', Rhea informed.

'Aye, but I think it's worth going to the consultation event, a week today, to let them know in person just how strongly we feel about it', John proposed.

'I'm with you on that one', agreed Murdoch.

'What time are you going? And is Jean going too?' asked Rhea.

'Aye, Jean will be there. We thought we'd head down for it opening about mid-day', John outlined. 'Do you want to meet here half an hour beforehand, and we can all go together?'

'Strength in numbers', Archie laughed, oblivious to the fact that if he had gone himself as a solitary presence, it would have communicated the very thing.

'Aye, strength in numbers Archie. It's important they see there is collective opposition to this', John suggested.

'Maybe we could ask Calum if we could put a petition on the bar, for people to sign, and take it along with us to the open day', proposed Rhea.

'The bugger would probably hide it behind the bar', smirked John, before adding that he thought it was, in fact, 'a fine idea'.

'There's over three thousand people who live on this island', Murdoch informed, ' and if we can get the majority of islanders to sign it, they will *have to* take our views into account'.

Rhea rose from her chair and went over to speak with Calum behind the bar.
When she returned, they all looked expectantly at her.
'He'll do it', she said.

When Jean arrived at the bar, she was appraised of what they were planning.

'What are you going to call us then?' asked Jean, only to be met by blank stares.
'Every action group needs a name', she insisted.

Archie, who had remained fairly quiet on the details of the planning proposal, up to this point, suggested, '"Pensioners against wind"'.

'Naw', said John smiling, 'that makes it sound as if we're against the natural elements. They'll just say they are trying to harness it, and do something useful with it'.

'What about "Pensioners against rotating turbines"', said Murdoch. 'At least it's more specific, and identifies just exactly what the problem is'.

'I think the fact that it says Pensioners, might be a turn off to some people', Jean piped in.

'Okay, I've got it', said Archie. 'There's five of us, so how about we call ourselves "the five against rotating turbines"'.

'That sounds too exclusive, Archie', said Rhea. 'It sounds as if it's just us five, when it should be open to all folk'.

'You're right', agreed Archie. '*Folk* against, it is'.

'Aye', said John, and no-one had any other objections, or, had any more ideas to add to it.

RESISTANCE

As was his custom, John awoke the next morning, rose from his bed, and looked out of the window.

Jean, was awake, for she was conscious her husband had been quite restless during the night.

'Did you not sleep well?' she asked, knowing the answer and pretty certain that she knew the cause.

'No', he said, as he dressed. 'I was thinking about this proposed wind farm', he confirmed.

'I thought you might be, dear', consoled Jean, knowing there would be no consoling her husband until a resolution was found.

'I'm going to nip up to the shop for the paper', he informed, and went downstairs where he found his long overcoat on the peg in the hallway.

It was a pleasant morning as he stepped outside and he walked up the Bria Road to the shop.

'Did you see in the Courier yesterday the Planning application to build six turbines up in Glen Bria, and on into the woods?' John asked. I don't like it', he informed.

'Aye, I saw that right enough', Mike replied.

'It'll be a disaster for the island', John suggested, as the shopkeeper listened to his customer become more animated.

'Is it the paper you're after?' Mike asked, holding the morning's Courier aloft.

'Aye and naw. I was wondering, Mike, if you'd be happy to keep a petition on the counter, for people to sign, registering their objections to the windfarm?' John asked.

'I…eh…don't know if I can do that', informed Mike, hesitantly.

'What do you mean, you don't know if you can do that?' asked John in disbelief. 'It's your shop'.

'But I don't want to put any of my customers off', Mike replied.

'How's it going to put anyone off?' John asked in disbelief. 'If they don't want to sign it, they can chose to ignore it'.

'Aye, that's true', Mike agreed, 'but I don't want anyone to feel pressurised into signing it'.

'But how are they going to feel pressurised?' asked John. 'It's not as if you are going to be bending their arm, or anything', he laughed in derision.

'Some people think it's a good idea', Mike suggested tentatively.

'How can they possibly think six giant blades on stilts, are a good thing for Bria and the island?' said John, shaking his head in disbelief.

'Well', proposed Mike, 'there's talk of a camp being built to house all the workers they will need to construct it'.

'And how's that a *good thing*?' asked John.

'Well for me, it might bring in good business, John. It's not easy trying to carve out a living in a village shop, you know', Mike informed.

'I get that, Mike. I really do', John responded. 'But once, or should I say, if it's built, there will be no bloody customers left to buy anything, cause they'll all have upped sticks and left the island. In fact, the only sticks that will be left, will be the six giant sticks with propellers stuck on them'.

'I don't know', said Mike, 'it might not be all that bad'.

'Did you not say to me yesterday, the shop has been in your family's hands for fifty three years?' John queried.

'Aye, that's right, nearly fifty three years, later this month', he confirmed.

'Well, you'll be lucky if it's here another fifty three weeks', said John vehemently, 'if that thing goes ahead'.

Just at this point another customer walked in.

'Good day', remarked Jim Soutter, nodding his head to the two men who were locked in a duel of words. John turned to greet him.

'Did you hear about the Planning application to build six turbines up in the Glen?' he asked.

'Aye', said Jim, with little more explanation which both men were eagerly waiting for.

'And what do you think about it?' asked John impatiently.

'Well', informed Jim with a big smile, 'it'll mean cheaper electricity for us all'.

'See', said Mike, feeling that his earlier point had just been proven.

'For goodness sake!' John exclaimed, and walked out the shop door without taking the newspaper he had come for with him.

Walking up the road he turned and followed the path enclosed by the overhanging trees.

He stood for a moment and surveyed the woods before him, shook his head, and walked on with a sombre face.

As he reached his home, having taken little in of his surroundings thereafter as his mind had been otherwise occupied, he was greeted by his wife.

'Was the paper not in yet?' Jean asked.

'Eh no, I forgot it', he replied curtly.

'That's not like you dear', she consoled. 'Would you like a cup of tea?' she offered.

He was going to decline out of sheer obstinacy, but checked himself in time.

'Yes, thank you', he replied.

When she returned with cup in hand, he recounted to her the earlier events at the shop.

'Well', said Jean, 'it's not the first time you've found that not everyone is on board'.

She was well aware of his frustration as a Union Steward, at just how often support for some action was rarely unanimous.

'True', he said. 'That's true', he repeated, deep in thought. 'I think I'll take the ferry over to the mainland, this morning', he advised.

'Whatever for?' asked Jean.

'I need to get a book from the library', he informed.

'Can you not wait till the van comes over?' she queried.

'It'll never have what I'm looking for', he stated quite emphatically.

Later that morning, he did take the small ferry over to the mainland. As he looked back at the island, with its sloping hills where Glen Bria stood, with its ancient forest before it turned into a dense modern forestry plantation, he felt a feeling of loss, which he always felt, when he was separated from his island home.

He caught the bus to the library, which was situated in the town which lay close to the ferry port. He hated this place. It had a run down appearance, with its shops boarded up with iron shutters, plastered with spray paint graffiti on them, the smell of petrol fumes from the cars, and the busyness of the people rushing to get to places all around him with no-one having the time or inclination to acknowledge one another. It seemed a cold, dark foreboding environment in which to live.

A group of youths with their black anoraks and hoodies, and with neck scarfs over their faces, stood with their electric bikes at a shop entrance. He walked past them and climbed the library steps.

Opening the parcel he had retrieved from the shop, it was with satisfaction that he found the templates with the design he had made, were a perfect fit for the transparent badge moulds he had purchased online.

Having sealed all thirty badges, he placed each of them in a box and then set about enlarging the image on his screen, into a large banner. He printed several of these in A4 size to fit placards they could carry and hold outside the Council Planning meeting.

But first, there was the community consultation event to attend at Clachan Village Hall, or what at least what was left standing of it.

ROAST

As the Councillor for the Dark Isle boarded the early morning ferry to the mainland, he went through to the ticket office.

'Return', he remarked, as he passed his money over the counter top.

'Thanks', he said, before slipping the ticket into his pocket and moving away from the small queue to take up position in the lounge by the square window.

It was cold and blustery outside, and the spray from the sea was hitting the side of the small ferry. He was restless, and decided instead to go outside on deck. It just didn't feel right, sitting inside while a chasm between the island and himself opened up.

Although not native to it, he had been brought up on the island from a very young age.

As the ferry pulled away he looked back at the silhouette of the island. As the engines rumbled from deep within the bowels of the ship's interior, he felt an inner sense of joy and excitement, as if he was being overcome by these emotions for the very first time.

The ferry gently bobbed up and down as it started its journey across the Sound, heading for the mainland, a familiar distance of only four miles.

As he looked back at the island, with its sloping hills, he felt a feeling of loss, as he usually did, when he was separated from his island home.

He knew, however, that he was one of the fortunate ones, for there were indeed few people of his own age who were now still on the island. There were few careers, aside from agriculture and tourism, and most of that was just seasonal in nature.

His friends had gone to University or College, and similarly he had followed the well-trodden path of the many who had gone before him, year after year, decade after decade.

But after completing his politics degree, he had managed to get a job at the local paper, which enabled him to return home to the island once more. Others however, had simply sailed across the Sound, never to return, but instead had crossed more expansive oceans and continents to seek life, liberty and the pursuit of happiness.

He reflected on events from over the years, of how his close friend had gone to see a Consultant, but that had been on the mainland. Of cousins who all seemed to have the better things in life, when they came to his house to visit them from the mainland.

Football teams who came and trounced them, from the mainland schools, and who had a much greater pool of players to choose from. Even at golf, those who came from over the sea, could match the best the island had to offer.

He stood on the deck and looked over the side of the ferry, and back towards the Dark Isle from where he had come.

'It has little to offer you', he recalled the remark from one of his teachers, which had run through his head as he watched the ferry push aside the waters like the hand of God, as jelly fish floated by.

He nodded in recognition of one of the lorry drivers who was also on deck, and who had come outside for a smoke.

'What you up to today?' asked the burly man, who had forearms the size of tree stumps.

'Off to visit a windfarm on the mainland', he informed.

'What for?' the man with Popeye sized forearms asked.

'To see the effects it has on the local area and the environment', he replied and was met with silence in response.

'I'm keen to ensure if they develop the one proposed for the island, that people's way of life is not affected detrimentally and that habitats are protected', he added by way of information.

'What…like the wildlife?' asked the driver.

'Yes, that the noise doesn't affect people, that property prices aren't adversely affected, that it doesn't deter tourists and that the forest and the wildlife are not spoiled, that sort of thing', he said adding, 'maybe one day people will see why we need to protect what we have, and hold onto what's dear to us'.

The lorry driver nodded and stubbed out his cigarette and returned indoors.
The Councillor stayed on deck.

He had long believed, and it was now beginning to gain acceptance, that the damage inflicted by humankind on the planet, was not only detrimental to many different species, but was ultimately detrimental to humankind itself.

It wasn't just species that were becoming non-existent due to dredging the seabed, or a distant rainforest where rapid deforestation was driving other species out of their natural habitat.
It was those who were already impoverished who suffered famine as a result of climate change.

It was also people who suffered the extremes of weather that long dry spells brought about, inevitably followed by the downpours which gave rise to their own specific problems, and it was people living on islands who bore the brunt of these changes, and who were having to evacuate their homes, due to rising sea levels.

Heaven forbid that such a thing should ever happen here, to the Dark Isle, his island, his home, he thought, as he looked at the land on the other side that was now coming more sharply into view.

The Dark Isle with its rugged hilly land on the north of the island, and flatter lands to the south, was in sharp contrast to the industrialised urban wasteland which lay on the other side of the Sound.

The island had an abundance of wildlife, birds of prey, red deer, otters, red squirrels, diverse sea life on the seabed, basking sharks, flora and fauna.

Oh yes, his island had journeyed through time as part of history, and was well deserving of its reputation. To him it was more reminiscent of heaven itself, if he had any way of knowing what that might look like.

He recalled the dances of his youth at the Clachan Village Hall, where youngsters looked upon one another from across the room, as if they were some sort of alien species; the dance floor constituting too vast an expanse of space to be safely conquered.

He recalled the walks up Glen Bria, where with each step, once you emerged from the tree line, you got one step closer to the celestial heavens, the nearer you got to the top.

On a small island, the dynamics and intensity of relationships could be studied closely, and gave a marvellous insight into human behaviour, doing much to aid his development in his formative years.

He felt that all that happened on the island was a microcosm of life itself.
He asked himself, how much more instructive could life be on the mainland than that?

'So you going to vote for it?'

Popeye had returned.

He offered the local Councillor a cigarette from an opened packet.

He hesitated, but then took one as if he was slowly drawing a card presented to him face down from a hidden deck.

'Thanks', he retorted, moving in to take a light from the dealer of the pack, and although the match had become lost he could just make out a faint glow amidst the dense forest of forearm hair.
He nodded his head in gratitude and took a long draw from the cigarette.

'Not so sure', he replied, spluttering in response to the initial verbal proposition as the cigarette smoke caught his throat.

'Will it bring jobs to the island?' asked the burly driver.

'Yes', he replied, 'If what they say is true'.

'What is truth?' retorted the Driver.

They stood for a while looking over the edge at the seagulls as they flew alongside the ferry.

Once again, the burly driver returned indoors while the Councillor remained on deck.
He watched as a rainbow appeared, crossing the sky from shore to shore.
Stubbing out his cigarette on the heavy iron floor of the ship's deck, he reminded himself more and more of the familiar haunts and the special places back home.

It mattered little if he was alone, as nature was there, always ready to entertain with some new delight, some new discovery.

Each day at his island home, was hardly the mundane trudge many of his friends complained of during the long winter months when he was younger.

Yes sure, there were storms, rain undoubtedly, days when there was no boat, but most of all it gave the island an atmosphere; an atmosphere that some found claustrophobic, yet made him feel exhilaration, which he found liberating.

'What is truth?' was the lorry driver's phrase that now ran through his head, as he watched the cars on the small rampway, lying in wait for the opportunity to savour all that the Dark Isle had to offer their occupants.

As the iron ramp of the roll on roll off ferry was lowered to enable them to begin disembarking, the cars were directed off first. The small ferry was full, as the first ferry in the morning to the mainland always was, or at least appeared to be when viewed when passing the pier.

His heart sank as he cast his view back towards the island, but he felt anew that inner sense of joy and excitement.
He could even still make out the hills of Glen Bria, as they gave one sharp last tug at his heart polarising his emotions.

He approached a car, where a man lowered its window and shouted to him.

'Are you ready for your trip, Sir?' he asked, as he exited the vehicle and opened the back door for his passenger

The Councillor looked at him.

'Thanks', he said, putting his briefcase on the backseat of the vehicle.

What is truth? he thought, unsure of whether or not the visit would be instructive or not in that respect.

He felt that there were things in life which could be found on the Dark Isle that were irreplaceable, more than any material benefits that could be sourced on the mainland.

The Dark Isle had journeyed alone through time and space and he was keen for it to continue on that journey too.

As he came to the Council Headquarters, he saw the bus, thanked the Council's driver, and boarded it.
There were a few Councillors still to arrive, and he acknowledged each one as they mounted the steep steps of the bus.

Before they set off, they were told it was a twenty minute journey to the site, and they were asked to review the information being sent around the bus.

As they drove through the town, with its graffiti on the iron rollers that adorned the front of some of the shops, with jargon and sexually explicit phraseology, a leaflet was handed to him.

Much to his surprise, it did not contain any information about the windfarm they were going to view, but instead was a menu for the Hotel they were set to dine in after the visit.

Roast Lamb

it simply read for the main course.

One of his colleagues popped his head over the headrest of the seat behind him.

'It comes with gravy', he informed. 'Plenty of gravy'.

SACCHARIN SWEETENERS

As had been agreed previously amongst them, the small group of protesters came together again, late in the morning of the Friday, before they travelled over the road to the Village Hall at Clachan to the community consultation event.

'I'm not really sure what to expect', said John, 'but I think it's important we let them know that each one of us is opposed to the scheme. I don't think we go as a collective body, as there is the danger they consolidate our protest as being an objection from one group. If we go as individual residents, it would be much more effective in sending them the message that we object and we are not alone'.

'I think as a strategy at this stage, you are right', Murdoch agreed.

'So, as much as I agree that you, Rhea, should be the spokesperson to any press interest on behalf of the group…'

There was general nodding of heads at this comment, and mumbles in agreement.

'…I don't think we should make any public statement at this time, in response to the proposal, as a campaign group. There might not even be any media attention at this stage anyway', John concluded.

'So, you won't be wanting the posters I have made up for today, or the badges then?' asked Archie, feeling a bit deflated.

'No, maybe hold onto them for the day of the hearing into the application, when we will protest outside the Council offices', John suggested.

'I brought them all with me. They are in the boot of the car, but I guess I'll just take them home with me until then', said Archie.

'You really are very talented', Jean consoled, and all nodded and mumbled their agreement.

'I think we listen to the arguments they put forward for the development, because only then will we able to counter them with facts', John advised.

'I've brought my notebook with me to take some notes', informed Murdoch. 'It's important to research what technical data they give us'.

'I think we'll leave that bit to you dear', laughed Rhea. 'All I know is that they will scar the landscape, which is enough for me. It was, after all, the landscape that drew us here all those years ago'.

'Indeed', agreed Murdoch.

'Do you all want to come in my car?' offered Archie.

Given Archie drove a Nissan Qashqai with a lot of leg room, and which Jean found hard to climb into given its height, all opted to take Archie up on his kind offer.

'Now, remember', said John, 'it's important we break up into smaller groups when we get there. We don't want them to think we are all together'.

'But we can't ignore each other', said Archie. 'That would look a bit strange, given we all live on the same island and know each other'.

'No, no. I don't mean that', said John trying to mask his frustration. 'Of course, we can say hello to one another. Just maybe don't speak to the same people at the same time as each other, that's all I'm meaning'.

'Oh', said Archie.

It was only a five minute drive over the hill to reach the village of Clachan.
There had always been a bit of inter-village rivalry between those who lived in Bria, and those who lived in Clachan, and who saw themselves as being the administrative capital of the island.

Most of the rivalry was just fun though, often spilling over at football matches between the two villages, or in other sporting events.

Bria was by far the better football team, but the fact that Clachan was where the secondary school was situated, as well as the island's police, ambulance station and one council office, alongwith the Doctor's surgery, meant the people of Clachan often thought they had some kind of claim to being the capital of the island.

However, more people stayed in Bria and that was also where the small ferry port was located, and which brought the many people and cars onto the island, particularly during the holiday seasons.

As Archie drove into the gravelled car park, where the Village Hall which had a badly run down appearance was situated, all noted that a few other cars were there too.

There was also a large van, with its company's name emblazoned on its side, and a big idyllic picture of a windfarm, set amongst some hills, as if in a remote Scottish Glen.

Beside the picture were the three faces, of a man, woman and child, presumably a modern nuclear family, all with smiles on their faces from ear to ear.

'Oh, the Highland paradise', remarked John sarcastically, but no-one really knew what he was referring to, and some thought he was being sarcastic either about Clachan, or about the state of the village hall itself.

Climbing out the car, which felt more like a jump for Jean, but yet one small step for Archie, they formed into their domestic couplings, except for Archie who followed on alone, and went in to the village hall in staggered formation.

'Welcome!' beamed the voice of a man who greeted John and Jean in the first instance. John couldn't help but notice the state of the wooden walls, part of one had a gaping hole in it, through which you could see the outdoors.

When he was younger, he had played five-a-side football in this very hall. Another inter-village rivalry event, but this time between neighbouring youth clubs. Needless to say, Bria had won that one too. He wondered if all the kicking of the ball against the walls, had loosened the wood panelling, plaster and brickwork behind it, over the years.

Their guide noticed John observing the state of the Hall, and didn't miss his opportunity.

'When we build the windfarm, of course there will be money to fix up the Hall, maybe even build a new one', he enthused.

'*If* you build a windfarm', corrected John, which served to put his guide on notice that he had an objector in his presence.

'Indeed, Sir. If the Council consent to the proposed plan to build the proposed wind farm, there will be *much* in the way of community financial benefit', he stressed in response.

'That may well be', retorted John, 'but is that a guarantee it will be spent exclusively on the island?'

'I don't have that detail', came the response. 'I think it would be for the Council to determine how the annual payments are allocated, Sir, so it may be your question is best directed to them'.

'And are they here, to answer that question?' asked John, looking around the room knowing the answer before he had asked it.

'No, Sir, but there is the Council meeting three weeks today in which to find out all these things', his guide proposed.

'If they will let us speak', remarked John.

'Well, Sir', the guide politely responded, 'you can also write to the Council expressing your views, which they will read and take into account, in determining any application that comes before them'.
There was a short pause.

'Why don't you come and look at the model and our brochure explaining it all, *before* you make your mind up?' he added.

'Yes dear, let's go and have a look', Jean suggested.

As Jean and John were herded over to a table, with a large scale model of the proposed windfarm, built on top of a wooden base, they were left in the company of a woman, while their initial welcomer returned to the entrance, just in time as Murdoch and Rhea made their entrance into the Hall.

'Welcome!' he beamed, in the same artificial tone of voice which a few minutes before had greeted John and Jean.

As John grew even more appalled at the sight of wind turbines towering over the trees of the woods of Glen Bria, albeit in matchstick model form, Murdoch was engaged in his own conquest.

'Will the trees in the Glen Bria woods not have to be felled, to accommodate the turbines?' asked Murdoch of his guide.

'No, Sir', answered the guide.

'But I just can't see how that can be', insisted Murdoch.

'Come, follow me and I'll show you on the scale model we have over here', the guide invited. Murdoch and Rhea followed on and were now standing around the table beside Jean and John, looking at the big square model that rested on it.

'Now, if you see here', he directed, trying to avert Murdoch's eyes onto the model turbines on the scale size model, before announcing proudly, 'you will see that the height of our turbines, that is 160 metres, tower way above the tallest of the trees'.

'Yes, but', interjected Murdoch, 'will the wind layers of air generated by the turbines not damage the trees?'

Jean, John, and his wife, Rhea, all stood there impressed by their friend's knowledge of the finite detail about wind turbines.

'Ah, but no, Sir', the woman at the table informed, the wind layers generated are also high above the tree crowns'.

Once again, the guide who had initially greeted the two couples on entrance to the Village Hall, returned to the entrance in anticipation of more arrivals.

This time Archie timed his entrance and went into the hall a few minutes thereafter.
Looking up at this rather tall figure of a man, the guide smiled with his all now too familiar opening of, 'Welcome!'

'Hello', said Archie rather timidly. 'Is this where I come to object to the windfarm?' he asked.

'Indeed, you can do that Sir, if that is your wish, but why don't you find out a little bit more about what is proposed first before you make up your mind?' suggested his guide in patronising overtones to his voice.

'But I'm against it', replied Archie, 'just as long as you know that'.

'Indeed, Sir', yawned the guide, before directing him over to the model of the proposed development.

'Hi!' said Archie to his co-conspirators, 'fancy meeting you here'.

John looked at him strangely.
'Hello Archie, how are you?'

Murdoch was still engaged in discussion with the woman from the renewables energy company at the table.

'So, you are saying that just one turbine will produce five to six million kilowatts of energy in a year, which will generate *more* than enough electricity for all the homes on the island?' he asked.

'Yes', said the woman, 'we estimate that it will power a thousand homes on the island'.

'So, why then do you need six of them?' he asked.

'Well, the ability to generate all that electricity, will enable any surplus to be sold back to the national grid. And what that means is…', she went on to outline, but Murdoch intervened.

'Is that it will need pylons to carry that energy, and a means of storing it?' he asked rhetorically.

'Yes, we can store surplus energy in batteries for later use, and we can also vary our supply to the national grid depending upon demands at any given time', she informed.

'But would that not require a subsea cable?' asked Murdoch, 'and would that not be a very costly option?'

'Well, you clearly have given this much thought', said the woman. 'But do remember the shortest point to the mainland is just a little over three miles, so although the cost of any subsea cable would be high, the small mileage would mitigate that. Anyway Sir', she concluded, 'these questions might be best answered by going through the brochures I am going to give you now. It has been delightful having so much interest in the proposed development, and we look forward to hearing the Council's decision in a few weeks' time'.

As they all exited the hall, except for Archie, who felt it was important not to be seen coming in or going out together, he rather sheepishly hung back, looking at the pictures of the turbines on the wall from other developments the company had built elsewhere.

When they all finally got in the car, when he decided to return, they were all quite subdued at first.

'That's one helluva' bigger development than what they are letting on publicly', Murdoch suggested.

'How do you reason that?' asked John with interest in his voice.

'Well, I'm no mathematician', said Murdoch which raised a smile unbeknown to him on everyone else's faces, 'but if one turbine generates enough energy, five to six million kilowatts, to power nearly all the houses on the island, then six will provide energy for the equivalent of somewhere between six and nine thousand homes'.

'That means', said John, 'that the energy is not so much to benefit the island, as it is to benefit elsewhere'.

'Exactly', said Murdoch. 'The more energy, the more money for the shareholders'.

'I wouldn't worry about there being six turbines', interjected Archie.

'Why naw?' said John highly irritated.

'Because now there's only five'.

Archie produced from his pocket, one of the small-scale wind turbines from the desktop model, and held it aloft.

All laughed heartily in childlike glee.

THE GRAVY TRAIN

The journey by coach to the windfarm was only about a thirty minute drive.

The towns which they passed through, some of which had previously been busy mining communities until the mid-80's, now just had a run down appearance, with few amenities and little employment opportunities in them.

But soon the coach was out on the countryside and began its steep ascent on the road up into the hills.

Before long, they had turned off, and were driving the short distance up the gravelled road, until they reached the entrance to the wind farm.

As they disembarked, they were met by Brian Whittington, who had given the presentation to the Council meeting.

'Good morning, Gentlemen', he said. 'I am so glad you could all join us on this glorious morning. Welcome to the Lochan Granda wind farm development'.

He handed each a brochure as they disembarked from the coach.

'I'm going to take you a walk around the site, and as I do so I am going to try and explain how the wind farm is set up and works. If there are any questions as we go through the development, please just stop and ask me'.

Brian led the group of twenty councillors around a small hillock.

'The wind turbines, which generate the electricity, are the most prominent feature of any windfarm, and here at Lochan Granda, the development comprises of four turbines which you can see, are located across the hillside in the distance.

This power that is generated, comes through cables laid underneath the ground, and into a substation. From there, there are more cables, known as interconnection cables, which are laid to reach the main road about a quarter of a mile from the substation, where they connect with the existing transmission system. Any questions at this stage, gentlemen?'

All were silent, but the island Councillor was restless.

'I can see how the turbines are brought to a site such as this, but how would you propose to bring them to the Dark Isle?'

'That is a very good question', replied Brian Whittington, trying not to sound too patronising. 'The idea', he continued, 'is to build a small marine port, which will also serve as a staging port, where the components of the turbines will be brought by sea, for the initial construction phase. This marine port will also serve as a maintenance base, once the windfarm is up and running'.

'But that will be quite an extensive development in itself', the island Councillor observed.

'Indeed, you are not wrong', conceded Brian, sensing this was an opportunity to take an open goal, 'but this will generate a lot of employment for the island and beyond'.

'Marvellous', remarked one of the mainland Councillors.

'Now you will observe gentlemen, that the turbines are placed between five and ten rotor diameters apart for optimal performance'.

'Can they not be placed any closer to one another?' asked one Councillor. 'Surely, this would help to minimise any visual impact'.

'The turbines need to be a certain distance from one another', Brian explained. 'Just like when you are flying, turbulence can affect the flight of the plane, so it is with turbines. They create turbulence in their wake, that's why we call it "wind wake", which means they can't be placed too close to one another. However, the good thing about an onshore windfarm, is that they are generally much smaller in size, and take up much less land, than an offshore development would do, helping to minimise the visual impact'.

'So, why do you only have four turbines here? Why not six, or, say ten or twenty?' asked another mainland Councillor.

'That's a really good question too', said Brian, before going on to explain that, 'the greater the number of turbines in a given area, the less efficient they are'.

The tour continued in the same vain, with questions and answers throughout, which Brian answered patiently and with clarity. He walked them to the top of the hill, and looking back at the other turbines, was able to explain in relation to their questions, that although there were only four turbines in this development, they were laid out in the shape of an isosceles trapezoid, to cover a specific area of land, in such a way, as to maximise the use of the area of land that the farm covered, while also maximizing their efficiency'.

After the walk up the hill, the Councillors were more than ready to be taken to the Amour Muck Hotel for their lunch.

No expense had been spared and on arrival, as they disembarked the steps of the coach, they were met by two waitresses carrying trays with champagne in flutes, which they readily consumed having worked up a thirst after their exertions.
Needless to say, drinking this rather too quickly led to a second.

As they stood in the courtyard, surveying the landscape and the rolling hills of the surrounding countryside, there was no noise to be heard from the windfarm which they had just visited.
In no time at all, the Councillors were beginning to feel a bit tipsy.

They were taken indoors and through to a grand dining room with several chandeliers, where a five course dinner had been laid on for them.

As they sat and marvelled at the windfarm they had just seen, at the information which Brian had so willingly imparted, and at the quality of the food which they were being served, they were soon enjoying the main course.

The Councillor for the island felt uneasy. He too had consumed his champagne all too quickly, having worked up a thirst, but amidst everyone else's enthusiasm, he felt all was not the rosy picture they had been painted.

'Roast Lamb', the waitress asked interrupting his thoughts, as the other waitresses delivered the plates to the long grand dining table.

This just doesn't feel right, he said to himself. 'Please', he replied.

'Would Sir care for some gravy?' the waiter asked, coming behind her.

'Yes, please', he said.

'Lots', said the next Councillor. 'Yes, lots of it'.

TWITCHERS

It was the following Friday, that John noticed Jean fumbling as her mobile phone rang. Her gentle slumber when sitting upright on the settee had been disturbed by its loud ringtone.

'Darn thing', she moaned aloud in exasperation, as she tried to answer it, using the smart screen function, initially with little success.

John said nothing. Out of conviction, he had a self-imposed prohibition on any snoozing during the daytime. Primarily, he knew if he did so, he just wouldn't sleep well, if at all, during the night. But more so, he remembered his father always coming home each evening after work, sitting in his chair, and then falling asleep. What a waste of time, he used to think to himself. He felt the same about people endlessly scrolling on their mobile phones.

Eventually Jean managed to manipulate the screen on her phone, enabling her to answer it.

'Hello, Jean speaking', she sang into the phone, the irritation in her voice from a moment ago having now lifted.

'Oh, hello Rhea', she exclaimed whilst walking through to the small kitchen to find some privacy.

As he too fumbled through the large sheets of that day's Courier, John came across a small article which said how in early May, the Royal Navy, as part of a N.A.T.O. exercise, would be conducting manoeuvres off the island and there would be activity in the bay.

That was not too unusual, for they had done so frequently in the past. Indeed, it was not uncommon to see submarines and navy frigates in the bay on occasions, as much of the submariners training was done in the waters around the island.

He recalled how when they had been visiting his eldest daughter, a few years back in the United States, where she lived, that they had been walking along the board walk next to the beach and the sea, when he noticed everyone had stopped walking, and were looking at the water.

He thought that maybe they had spotted a shark. But no, as it turned out, they were all looking at a U.S. navy submarine, which was for them quite a rare sight. He was more in awe of all the planes and helicopters that seemed to fly overhead at a moment's notice, whereas the residents of that seaside city, seemed oblivious to them.

At least when they would visit Jeanette, his youngest daughter, who stayed on the west side of the island here at home, there was next to no noise where she lived. In fact, there was next to no one in the village there at all.

He recalled the last occasion, when the navy had come ashore, how the peace had been shattered, when a melee had broken out at the hotel bar one night, when several of the sailors had got drunk and had started a brawl. They had caused quite a bit of damage, but little did they know that on the other side of the island, the Parliamentary Under Secretary of State for the Armed Forces had his holiday home. He just happened to be holidaying on the island when the melee broke out, and as happens on islands, news was quick to spread, and he soon heard about this debacle which had disturbed the peace on the island.

Much to the surprise of the Captain of the ship, from which the sailors had come, he had been roused from his slumber by the Ministry of Defence, demanding that he bring his sailors under control.

In fairness to him, he had done so, lining all his men up on deck, identifying the perpetrators, fining and even reducing the rank of one, before sending a party of sailors to the island to make reparations and make good the damage they had done.

Jean returned from her call in the kitchen, and was trying to end it by swiping her finger across the screen of the smartphone.

'Life used to be so much simpler when we all had land lines', she grumbled. Having managed to complete the task she was trying to do, she lifted her head and as her eyes lit up, she simply said, 'Interesting news'.

'Oh, what's that dear?' John enquired.

'That was Rhea', she replied.

'Yes, I heard you', said John.

'Ah, but you didn't hear what she was saying, now did you?' Jean retorted.

'Eh no, but go on', he replied.

'Well', she said, 'you will never guess what Rhea saw?'

'No, you are right dear, I'll never guess what Rhea saw'.

'Well, she saw an owl', Jean informed.

'Oh, that's nice dear. How exciting for her', John remarked, but his response sounded rather sardonic.

'Don't be so sarcastic, you grumpy old man', she shot back, 'or I won't tell you then'.

'Tell me what?' he asked slightly chastened.

'Rhea saw, well it wasn't her who saw it, but one of the schoolchildren reported they had seen a Snowy Owl up in Glen Bria'.

'Oh wonderful', John sang in reply. 'How exciting for them'. He realised that sounded just as sarcastic in tone.

'Don't you see?' asked Jean.

'See what dear?' he asked.

'It was a snowy owl', Jean replied emphatically.

John looked down again at his newspaper, before lifting his head again to reply.

'Yes, are they not white or something?' he asked, unsure at what she was driving at.

'Not that you'd know', she replied critically. 'And the reason you wouldn't know John, is because you will never have seen one, will you now?'

'I've maybe seen them in books or on T.V., but no, I don't ever recall seeing one up close and personal', he advised.

'I'm not surprised', said Jean before asking, 'do you know how many snowy owls there are in the country?

'I don't know', he said lifting his head again from the newspaper.

'Guess', she instructed.

'A few hundred, a few thousand perhaps?' he asked feigning interest.

'Three', she replied.

'What, three thousand?' he asked.

'No, three, as in three fingers', she informed him, holding them aloft to reinforce the point she was making.

'Well, goodness gracious me', said John, trying but failing not to sound sarcastic this time.

'Don't you see?' exclaimed Jean.

'See what, Jean?' asked John, the pitch of his voice rising, unsure of what it was he was meant to be seeing or understanding.

'If there are only three snowy owls, they're exceptionally rare'.

'True', said John.

'And if they're exceptionally rare, they are protected, John', she concluded.

'So?' said John, before his moment of awakening. 'You mean, if they are protected, they cannot be interfered with'.

'Yes, that's what protected generally means', said Jean being the sarcastic one on this occasion.

'And if they are protected', said John, 'their habitat cannot be disturbed, is that not right?'

'I think that's right John', she agreed. 'But we need a way of showing that they are there, in Glen Bria'.

'Yes, yes', said John rising to his feet and discarding the newspaper on the chair behind him. 'Maybe we could take a picture of one, and present it at the Council meeting at the end of next week. Mind you, do they not only come out at night?' he asked.

'According to Rhea, Murdoch who is a bit of an ornithologist…'

'Is there nothing that man doesn't know about?' jested John.

'Yes, according to Rhea, he said that unlike other owls, they are best spotted before dawn and after sunset', Jean informed.

'Well, that's it then', said John, 'we will organise a search party for this week. We will go there one evening, and see if we can capture it'.

'Oh, you can't do that dear', said Jean alarmed.

'No, I mean on camera', John clarified.

'That's a great idea love', said Jean.

'We have just over a week to find it', he concluded.

'Surely, we will find it', said John to both Archie and Murdoch, as he supped his half pint that evening in the pub.

'What do you say, we go out this time tomorrow night at say seven o'clock?' Murdoch proposed. 'We've still got a week before the clocks change, so we can walk up the Glen and by the time we get near the top, it'll be twilight and just beginning to get dark'.

'I've got the zoom lens on my camera', Archie chirped in. 'Even if it's a bit far off, I should be able to capture it'.

'Excellent', said Murdoch.

At this point, Calum was at their table, having made one of his rare excursions from behind the bar, to collect their empty glasses.
'So, what have you guys got on this week?' he asked out of genuine interest.

'We're off to see some birds tomorrow night', Archie informed.

'Will both of your missuses no mind?' laughed Calum, turning to look at Murdoch and John. 'It's aw'right, your secret's safe wi' me', he laughed.

'Very witty', retorted John acerbically.

'I wiz' only joking', said Calum. 'Try and lighten up a bit John, it won't do you any harm once in a while'.

'Well, if people would show some interest in this wind farm and the impact it might have on the island, maybe I could smile a bit more', said John.

'You still on about that?' asked the bartender.

'Well, someone has got to be. The sad thing about it all, is not so much whether anyone is paying attention to it, or not, it's whether anyone will care enough, to do something about it', John shot back all serious in demeanour.

'Here then, I've got something that will make you smile', said Calum and he turned around and headed back to the bar.

'What's he going to do?' asked Archie. 'Get us another drink?'

'Nah, not him', said John.

Calum returned and from behind his back produced a clipboard.

'What's that?' asked John.

'It's the petition your Rhea, Murdoch, asked me to start behind the bar'.

'And has *anyone* bothered to sign it?' John asked.

'Look', said Murdoch, 'the page is full'.

'What's that?' asked John, ' fifteen, maybe twenty signatures on it?'

'Aye, that's right', said Calum.

'There's over three thousand people that live on this island…', remarked John in disgust, but before he could finish his sentence, Calum turned the sheet over, and then over and over again.
'There must be about ten or fifteen pages there Calum!' John gasped.

'Aye, you're right there', said the bartender, 'there are fifteen pages with twenty signatures on each, that's…'

'Three hundred', interjected Murdoch.

'That's great!' exclaimed John. 'How did you manage that then?'

'I just said to each new customer over the last few weeks, if you want to drink in this bar, you will have to sign this. And they did'.

'Oh, well done that man', said Murdoch and John smiled.

'Told you I'd something that would make you smile', and with that parting comment, Calum returned to the bar.

'That's pretty damn good', said Archie.

'A tenth of the island', informed Murdoch.

'So, there *is* support', said John feeling some relief and justification for all that had passed. 'Well let's go tomorrow night and catch those birds', he exclaimed all enthused.

They all agreed to meet at Archie's house the following evening at seven o'clock, as he stayed closest to the Shee Gate, which gave access to the Glen.

As he went to leave the pub, John went over and bought Calum a drink.

'Cheers', said Calum.

TWIT TWOO

The very next evening, John appeared in the living room with his binoculars around his neck.

'You very much look the part', said Jean mockingly, 'but will they be much use when it gets dark?'

'No, probably not', John replied.

'Why not take the torch?' Jean suggested.

'Good idea', said John going through the doorway which led to the kitchen. When he returned a moment later, he had the torch in hand. He switched it on.

'Have we not got any batteries in this house?' he asked frustrated.

'That's your Department dear', Jean retorted. 'Why, is it not working?' she asked.

'It's fine', he informed. 'It's just a bit flickery. But it'll do', he said.

'Here, take my phone too, in case you need it', she replied.

As he walked up Bria Main Road towards Archie's house which lay near to the Shee Gate, which opened into the woods, and which led to a field serving as an access point to Glen Bria, he looked at his watch nervously.
A search for batteries before he had left the house had proved fruitless. He was conscious that the flickering torch might not survive any sustained use but he was also anxious that he should not be late.

It wasn't that Archie or Murdoch wouldn't have waited for him, it was more he had a self-imposed rule about always being punctual and had never been late for anything in his life.

Getting to the door of Archie's house slightly out of breath, having walked uphill and at a faster pace than normal, he looked at his watch with some satisfaction, which read five minutes to seven. He chapped on the lounge window and opened the door.
Walking through to Archie's living room which the main door of his cottage opened into, he saw Archie standing there with a large camera around his neck.

'David Bailey eat your heart out', he remarked to his tall friend.

'You think I look the part?' asked Archie.

'The length of that lens is almost as long as you are, Archie', John exclaimed. 'Here, let's have a look'.

Archie took the camera from around his neck and passed it to John.

'Blinkin' heck', said John not expecting it to be so heavy, 'that weighs a bloody tonne man. If I was to go up the Glen with that round my neck, I'd be lucky to get as far as the Shee Gate'.

Archie laughed, for the Shee Gate lay only about another hundred yards up the road from his house. He was also oblivious to his own strength, as well as presence, and never gave the weight of the camera and its long lens a moment's thought.

Just then Murdoch popped his head around the door.

'I see you both have come equipped', he remarked, looking at the camera and John's torch sticking out his jacket pocket.
'Seven o'clock exactly', he said. 'Shall we go?'

The three men exited the main door, Archie ducking as he opened the door, and which he did not lock behind him. He had never done so, and never thought to do so now. In fact, having been his parents' house, neither of whom had ever locked the door either, it was very likely the door had in fact never been locked. Whether Archie even had a key to do so, would be anyone's guess.

As they entered the Shee Gate and walked on a few yards, they were struck by just how much darker it was amidst the cover of the trees. In fact, John was unsure whether or not they might in fact need to use the torch, sooner rather than later. He knew it would not last the half hour it would take to reach the opening to the field that opens out into the expanse of the Glen.

They had also chosen a moonless night, which might not help their cause.

Sensing his friend's concern, Murdoch assured them that once they reached the access point to the field, they would leave the cover of the trees behind, and it would still be light enough to continue their walk up the Glen to reach its higher points.

As they walked past the wooden posts clad in ivy, giving them the appearance of wise old men who were watching their every move, and who were deep in contemplation, they soon heard the mumbling of the river and came across the lochan.

'We used to fish in there when we are at school, remember?' said Archie turning to John.

'I never caught a thing', said John with laughter in his voice.

'But there were always the mussels that could be had', consoled Archie.

'What, you get mussels in there?' asked Murdoch surprised.

'Oh yes', informed Archie. 'I think they are called *pearl* mussels. Mind you, we never found a pearl in them to this day'.

'Well, you learn something new every day', said Murdoch smiling. 'I've heard of pearl mussels, but I never knew they could be found here in freshwater. I thought you only got mussels in the sea'. Archie was pleased he knew something which Murdoch didn't. It was indeed a rare moment to savour.

As the three men progressed along the path it was getting darker. One tree appeared skeletal and in the shape of an old woman with crooked limbs for branches. Just then there was a noise.

'Bloody hell!' said Archie jumping about the same distance in the air as his ginormous seven feet in height.

'It's only a bleedin' horse', said John slightly irritated by his friend's unnecessary fearfulness.

Murdoch roared in laughter.

Despite being built like a horse, and giving some of the younger trees a run for their money in terms of height, Archie was probably the softest man you might ever meet.

He was certainly not the kind of figure you would want to meet alone in the wood on a dark evening like this one was, but the truth was he would be the first one to get spooked and run the other way.

John often remembered when at school, the visiting school football teams to the island, often looked upon Archie with some fear in their eyes. That was before the whistle to start the match was sounded, then the truth was exposed.

On one such occasion, the school football pitch had been rather waterlogged the day before, and a few puddles remained on the pitch when the match kicked off the next day.

Running to get the ball before his opponent got it, Archie was first to reach it, but finding it sat in the middle of a big puddle, and much to his opponent's amusement, Archie pulled himself up sharply to a halt. He would not go in to the muddy puddle, and his opponent was able to retrieve the ball and take it out of his reach.

The headteacher, who was the coach of the island's school football team, just smacked his head in sheer frustration.

'That made me jump', said Archie, somewhat relieved to hear it was only the neighing of a horse.

'You don't say', remarked John sarcastically.

It was about thirty minutes after they had set off from the big man's house, when they reached the ancient monolithic stones with their unique markings, just a few yards off the track.
Behind the stones, as viewed from the track side, lay a small opening to a field. A small sign also pointed to a new track, which the three men now took.

Once through the opening, they found themselves in the Glen and at the bottom of some hills. It was indeed a bit lighter without the cover of trees, though a small copse could still be found for the first hundred yards or so, from the entrance to the Glen.

'I would have thought snowy owls would have preferred to live in the trees', said Archie looking back at the tree line of the wood.

'You would have thought so', said Murdoch, 'but surprisingly they make their nests on the ground. This is the best time of day for seeing them, as they go hunting, so keep your eyes and ears wide open'.

Despite the peak time of the evening for spotting them, and with still about an hour until full darkness set in, the men had used the twilight hours to walk up to the top of the hills without seeing anything, and returned disappointed.

But then, just as they were approaching the tree line to the woods, Archie grabbed Murdoch's arm and pointed to a bird in the sky.

As the three men watched, it flew low just above the tree line, before landing and perching on a tree.

Murdoch reached a neighbouring tree and began to climb it, in the hope of getting a closer look. Once he had reached the top, he waved his hand, which Archie thought was a signal to climb the tree with his camera to take a shot.

Mounting the tree, his heavy build caused it to shake violently, as he clambered up in great excitement. The effect of this sudden movement caused Murdoch, who was slightly higher up, to overbalance, and down he came landing flat on his back and onto the hard ground.

'Bloody hell!' he shouted, as he writhed in pain on the ground, clearly winded.

'Oh, my goodness', said John running over to see if he was okay. Archie clambered down the tree, before dropping a few feet to the ground, which was easy for him to do.

'My back, my back', cried Murdoch, holding the lower right hand side of his back.

'Try and keep still, if you can', said John while Archie looked down at the sad figure rolling about on the bracken.

'Did you see it?' he asked.

'What?' asked Murdoch still clearly in pain.

'The owl, the snowy owl', said Archie impatiently.

'No, no, oh my back', cried Murdoch, 'it was…it was a bloody seagull'.

Both John and Archie laughed, and even Murdoch could see the funny side, but the pain kept him from laughing too.

'Can you stand up?' asked John.

Murdoch tried to raise himself from the ground, but fell back on to it holding his back. *'Ouch!'* he cried, 'I don't think so'.

'What we gonna' do?' asked Archie panicking unhelpfully.

'I don't know', said John in deep thought. 'I do know, we'll have to call the mountain rescue'.

'The mountain rescue', said Archie disbelievingly. 'Why the mountain rescue?'

'Because they will never get an ambulance up here', said John. 'And even if we got him down to the track in the woods, that track is just a bit too narrow to take an ambulance'.

'How will we get the mountain rescue?' Archie queried.

'I feel a right bloody twit now', Murdoch remarked, clutching his back.

'I've got Jean's phone', informed John reaching into his inside pocket. As he retrieved the phone, he switched it on and then fumbled with the screen as he tried to make the call from it. He then appreciated Jean's difficulty using it, as the more he tried to switch on the call function, the less it seemed to respond to his touch. Composing himself and taking a deep breath, he finally held the phone to his ear.

'Mountain Rescue please', he said.

ROTARY BLADES

Archie, who wasn't usually too vocal or expressive about anything, explained to Rhea that it had been just as well that the mountain rescue had been called, as they soon realised on reaching Murdoch, that no vehicle could reach him, nor transport him safely to Clachan, where the local Cottage Hospital was located.

In fact, with a potential back injury and given the complicated location of where Murdoch had fallen, the Mountain Rescue Team Leader had advised that a helicopter to fly the casualty to the mainland, was the only real practical solution to the problem facing his team.

It was not uncommon for the air ambulance to be called to the island, more often than not, to take casualties who had fallen on the hills, to the hospital on the mainland that was designated for that purpose.

Despite Murdoch's disdain for all things rotary, all he really could recall of the incident, when his wife visited him the next morning in the hospital, was the heavy and deep rhythmic breathing of the helicopter's blades as it took off, or as it was flying through the air.

He had been given some strong painkillers, either after, or before, he had been put onto a scoop stretcher, which is used for patients with suspected back injuries, and could remember little of the events leading up to his fall or his flight.

'It's just like you, Murdoch', chastened his wife, although she was greatly relieved to find him in good spirits and generally in good health too. 'You've always got to throw yourself right into the thick of things'.

'I think I was thrown *from* the thick of things from what they say', he laughed. 'What's the point of doing anything anyway if you are only going to do it half-hearted?' he concluded.

'The Doctor says it's likely you have only broken some ribs, which will heal of their own accord in time, but they won't know for sure until they do the x-ray later today'.

'That's right dear. They said if that doesn't prove conclusive, then I might also have to have a CT scan. If you ask me, it's all a lot of fuss about nothing'.

'Just as well they don't ask you', Rhea grimaced. 'I am glad I am here to keep them right'. Murdoch raised his eyes in resignation.

'Oh, it's not a lot of fuss about nothing', his wife glowered at him. 'It's your health, for goodness' sake. The Doctor said to me they need to do a proper x-ray, as the concern he has is that you still have some neck pain and seem to be a bit confused about what happened'.

'I'm not surprised love', retorted Murdoch, 'if I fell out of a tree, as they said, then I probably sprained my neck in the fall, that's all'.

The next day, when John and Jean had visited Rhea at her home, they were relieved to hear from her that no major injuries had been found following Murdoch's x-ray. Despite there being no evidence, other than the one possible sighting by a school pupil, of any snowy owls living in Glen Bria, Murdoch had remained in good spirits throughout his hospital stay.

'Yes, they think it is just some broken ribs on the side where he fell', she informed her visitors. 'They want to keep him in for the week for observation though, just to be sure, given his age'.

'But that'll mean he'll miss the Council meeting!' John exclaimed in horror.

'John!' shouted Jean in disgust at her husband's response.

'Oh, don't worry Jean. When the Doctor broke the news to Murdoch, he said *exactly* the same thing,' Rhea informed.

'No, I don't mean that Rhea. Of course, I want him to be fit and in good health. He gave me quite a fright that night if I'm honest with you'.

John stopped for a breath, and regaining his composure continued.

'I just mean he's got such a technical mind. You both heard him for yourself at the consultation meeting', said John despairingly.

'I know, John', consoled Rhea. 'I'm just glad you had the good sense to phone the mountain rescue or goodness knows how long he would have been lying there waiting for help. He says he'll go through things with me next week, so that if there is a press statement to be made it will sound technically accurate'.

'That's good, that's good', said John repeating himself. 'He will be missed on the day by us all'.

'Yes, I'm sure that's true', Rhea responded. 'But if there are any questions beforehand, just ask him when you go over and see him, or if something jumps to mind, ask me to ask him for you when I go over'.

'Yes, good idea', said John. 'I've been permitted to make a three minute address at the Planning meeting, as a representative of our group. It would've been great to have him with me, just to pick up on any last minute things that might be said by anyone in the Chamber that were technically wrong, so that we could point it out, but it really doesn't matter'.

Although Rhea would not collect her husband from the hospital until the Monday after the meeting, she confirmed that she would still definitely be attending. She would be outside the Chamber with the demonstrators, and would speak to the press, whether that be the local Courier, radio, or even the regional television station should it send someone to cover the protest and the Hearing.

'I've certainly made them all aware of it', she informed. 'Archie says he has made up badges for all those who attend, to wear on the march to the Council chamber, and he has also printed off some sheets for people to put on the placards'.

'Placards?' asked John, unsure of how they would source these.

'I got Willie, the joiner, to make several dozen. He'll meet us at the pier and give them to each person who will carry them. It's only a short walk to the Council chamber when we get to the other side anyway', Rhea informed.

'Yes, that's true', said John. 'I still feel somewhat aggrieved that such a big decision affecting the island, is not going to be made on the island. That meeting should at the very least have been held here'.

'Yes', both women agreed.

BREAKING WIND

Brian Whittington got up early on that Friday morning. He went down for breakfast in the hotel his employers had put him up in. They really spared no expense on his comfort, he thought, and considered himself lucky to have the job he had.

Mind you, he was ready for the day ahead and well-rehearsed for the Council planning meeting.

Indeed, this was probably the twelfth meeting of this nature that he had attended. Nine had been successful, one rejected, and one called in for an Inquiry before it was finally approved. He was quite pleased with his track record, as was his employer.

Each Council had their own way of doing things, and the Council's procedure here, with a few tweaks here and there, was broadly similar to most of the Planning Application meetings he had attended.

The Chairperson of the committee would introduce the application. Then the Council's Planning Officer would outline in more detail the extent of the proposal, and any additional information that relates to it, before concluding with a recommendation of whether or not to approve the application, and grant a licence. This recommendation is advisory only, but carries great weight, though the final decision rests with the Council Planning committee.

Then interested parties who have representatives are invited to address the committee, those for and those against, and then Brian would be invited to address the committee, which usually enabled him to debunk the crazies, and those with more informed arguments.

Then, the local Councillor, for the island in this instance, would be called upon to make comments.

Generally, they were allowed three minutes to make their comments to the Committee, before the Committee would deliberate on their decision, in light of the Planning Officer's recommendations and the arguments which they had heard put before them.

He had heard the arguments so many times before. Indeed, when initially invited to talk about the application, when he had invited them to the site tour which they had all taken him up on, most of the same arguments that he would hear today, would have been raised then. As a result, he was forearmed and prepared for whatever might be thrown at him.

Unlike the first few Hearings which he undertook when he was new to the role, no longer was he as anxious and obsessed about every word that he might say.

He had said them so many times before now, that he could almost regurgitate them in his sleep.

John wakened early and rose from his bed, looked out of the window, and simply remarked,

'I don't like this'.

Then he realised Jean was not in bed, which he found most strange, as he was always the first one to get up most mornings.

He went downstairs, and when he reached the bottom of the stairs, he heard retching coming from the toilet under the stairs. It was Jean.

'What's the matter, love?' he cried through the door.

'Oh, go away', she replied before retching again.

'Do you need me to phone the Doctor?' he asked, mindful that it would be another hour before the surgery opened. Then he remembered the boat left only half an hour after that, which would be cutting things fine.

'No, no', she replied. 'Just let me be. I'll be fine', she said.

'Well, you don't exactly sound fine, love', he remarked.

'No, on you go, you've got a big day ahead of you. Go and get some breakfast', she shouted.

'I can't leave you like this, now can I?' he shouted back.

She opened the door.

'Were you sick?' he asked.

'No, no, nothing like that. I've just got a stomach ache', she informed. 'Look, I'll be fine. But I don't think I'll make it to the protest, but I'll be fine'.

John stood there thoughtful before walking through to the kitchen. He wondered what he should do. It wasn't like Jean to be ill.

He made himself a cup of tea and listened out for his wife's movements. She had gone back upstairs to bed. He made another cup of tea and went upstairs.

'I've brought you some tea', he said presenting it in mid-air as he entered the bedroom.

'Just put it down on my side table', Jean replied.

'I can always get Archie to make the address to the Council', he suggested. 'I could stay here with you until you see the Doctor'.

'Don't be silly', said Jean. 'You've been preparing for this day for weeks now. You can't let everyone down'.

'But I can't just leave you here', John retorted.

'Yes, you can, and you will John. Look, the protest has already lost Murdoch's input for today. That's bad enough, but you are the figurehead for the campaign. How devastating a blow would that be for everyone who turns out today, if you don't turn up?'

John did not reply, but put the cup of tea on the bedside table as Jean had requested.

He went downstairs and grabbed his notes, and started to speak them aloud in the sitting room, as if he was presenting them to the Council Planning meeting. But he could not concentrate.

After a while, stopping and starting, he picked up Jean's mobile phone. He hung on the phone for ten minutes waiting for a response, but gave up. Then he phoned another number, but hung up because there was no response from that one either.

He returned to his notes and gave his speech to the mirror hanging on the wall. He was conscious that time was going on, but he really felt he could not leave Jean in the house like this and then the mobile phone rang.

Looking at the screen, his fingers fumbled in a few attempts to answer the call before finally doing so.

'Hello', he said.

'Dad', came the voice on the other end of the phone. 'You phoned', she said.

'How did you know I phoned you?' he asked bemused.

'Because it says so on my phone', she replied, shaking her head at the older generation's level of technological aptitude.

'Your mother's not too well this morning, and I don't want to leave her alone', he advised.

'But you've got the Council meeting', his youngest daughter Jeanette replied. 'You can't miss that. Everyone on the island is relying on you'.

'Blimey, the weight of expectation', he replied sarcastically.

'Look, I'll come over', she said. 'My shift finished half an hour ago, and I'm just on my way home to go to bed'.

'Are you sure, love?' he asked.

'Yes', she said. 'I'd just be sleeping at home anyway. Now get down to that pier. I passed a group of people heading for the ferry, when I drove past about fifteen minutes ago', she informed.

'Seriously?' he asked disbelievingly.

'Seriously', she said. 'There were the crofters, all in a group together. Anyway, best not to stay on the phone too long, Dad, or you'll miss the boat. Just go down there and see for yourself. I'll be over shortly'.

John felt quite heartened that a group of crofters felt strongly enough to come and join the protest. Many had indeed been vocal to him about how it was their land, but not just their land, but a way of life that was being put at risk by the proposed development.

He went upstairs, put his head around the door, and found Jean was sleeping. He took his suit jacket from the wardrobe, put the mobile phone on her bedside table, and went to kiss her on the forehead, but thought better of it, in case he wakened her. Quietly he shut the bedroom door and descended the stairs. Opening the front door of the cottage, he looked skywards and counted his blessings that it was not raining. The clocks had gone forward and this was the season for April showers.

The pier was only a fifteen minute walk from his house. Some cars passed him on the road there, undoubtedly ferry bound, for life on the small island seemed to revolve around the ferry which was after all a lifeline service.

As he walked round the bend, he knew it was only about another five minutes before he would reach the entrance to the pier. The closer he got to the entrance, he started to hear a rumble.

What could it possibly be? he asked himself, and when he reached the top of the road opposite the pier entrance, he looked down at what he could only describe as being a sea of people. He couldn't ever recall seeing so many people outwith the holiday season on the island, all gathered together in such close proximity to one another.

He walked down the small road and saw big Archie, towering above everyone else, at the entrance to the piermaster's office.

'Archie!' he shouted as he pushed his way through the throng. Eventually, he got to the front, where Archie was standing with Willie the Joiner.

'What's on?' he asked.

'What do you mean *what's on*?' asked Archie.

'Is there something on, on the mainland today, that I don't know about?' John clarified.

'They're all here for your protest', said Willie.

John looked around him in disbelief. He knew most of the faces. That's what happens when you live on an island.

There were the crofters in one group, just as Jeanette had said on the phone. There were the Carmichaels from Clachan. There was Calum, the bartender, who came over to talk to him.

'Look what I've got', he said, presenting a small folder which he gave to John.

'What's this?' asked John.

'It's a twenty five page petition, John. Five hundred signatures and all and all', he smirked.

John looked stunned.

'What are you looking so surprised at John?' he smiled. 'I live on the island too, you know'.

John was even more surprised, to see Mike, the shopkeeper, standing talking to one of the crofters.

'Do you think he's here for the march?' John asked Archie.

'Aye, he is that', confirmed Archie. 'They're *all* here for the march, John'.

John looked around. He estimated that there must have been around two hundred, maybe two hundred and fifty people on the pier. He wondered how the little ferry would cope. Then his mind turned to other practical matters.

'What happened to the placards and badges you were going to give everyone, Archie? he asked.

'I've got them all in the box here, and Willie has all the placards in the back of his van. I'll give people the badges as they disembark on the other side, and Willie will attach the posters I've made to the placards and give them to those who want to carry one, as we march on the Council office'.

'Excellent', said John.

They were joined by Rhea who had struggled to get through the crowd.
'Gosh, what a crowd', she exclaimed.

'It's great, isn't it?' said Archie, but John, delighted as he was, increasingly felt the weight of expectation on his shoulders and felt increasing anxiety. He felt for the packet of fudge in his pocket.

'Is Jean not with you?' asked Rhea.

'No, she's been sick throughout the morning', John informed.

'She'll be gutted to miss this', said Rhea.

'Aye', said John, thinking about the speech he'd written and saying bits of it over and over in his head. 'She has bad guts', he said glibly.

As the ramp on the small ferry lowered onto the slipway, the crew guided the five cars and Willie's van on board. Then they waved to the passengers to come aboard.
As the capacity was for only one hundred and fifty passengers at a time, it meant about one hundred were left behind.

'That's a shame if they don't get there', remarked John.

'Och, don't worry about that', said Willie the Joiner. 'I'll be at the other end with the placards, and will see the next lot when they come off the boat. They will still have ten minutes to get up to the Council Chamber. I reckon they will get there just in time for it starting'.

'You'll be inside anyway', said Archie. 'Let us worry about the rabble. We'll make sure they make plenty noise'.

Rabble was a good description, for the twenty five minute journey across the Sound was a boisterous affair. John gave up rehearsing his speech in his head, he just couldn't concentrate.

Instead, he thought about Jean and hoped that his youngest daughter, Jeanette, had made it round to the house from the other side of the island.
She was a carer in the Care Home on the island, and she would know what to do and what would be best for her mother.

As the boat neared the mainland, the rumble of the engines gave way to a siren that indicated the ramp was going to be lowered.

The purser on the ferry was still issuing tickets as it docked, as it was unusual at this time of year, before the holiday season had begun, to have this many passengers on board.

The vehicles were waved off first, and Willie drove up the slipway and parked his van up beside the entrance to the walkway.

Archie made sure, which was not difficult given his size and stature, that he was the first one off the ferry and made his way up towards the van.

As the passengers made their way up the slipway and came to the start of the walkway which was separated from the cars who were waiting to get on the ferry, Archie gave each a badge. Several took one of the pieces of paper Archie also gave them, and Willie quickly stapled each one to the wooden placards he had made.

When John, who was near the end of the crowd of passengers disembarking finally reached Archie, he was joined by Rhea.

'Here', said John, 'give me one of the badges for wearing in the Council chamber'.

Archie handed him one.

Both John and Rhea looked at it, then at each other.

'Archie, *what's this?*' exclaimed John.

'Do you like it?' asked Archie encouraged.

'Well, eh, no. Sorry to disappoint you, Archie. I don't, I really don't', said John.

'I've tried to capture the sea around the island with a dark blue background and white ripples for waves,' he said defensively, 'and I put a big wind turbine bang on the middle of the island'.

'Yes, that's great Archie, and I'm not trying to hurt your feelings, but…', said John.

'What is it then?' Archie asked a bit hurt and confused.

'You've put in big bold letters, the word **F.A.R.T.** around the edge of it', remarked John with a gasp.

'But that's exactly what we agreed that night in the pub', exclaimed Archie.

'Wait a minute', said John, 'I don't remember no fart'.

'No, no, we did. We decided the action group would be known as Folk Against Rotary Turbines. We did', he stressed.

John looked thoughtful.

'Yes, we did, so how did you get F.A.R.T.?' he asked, before answering his own question. 'Oh, I see. It's an acronym'.

'Yes, that's right', said Archie feeling justified, 'whatever you call it. I just couldn't fit the full name around the perimeter of the badge, so I had to condense it into something that fit neatly around it'.

'But did you not think about it first, Archie?' said John in disbelief. 'Here, let me see the poster, Willie'.

Willie handed John and Rhea a poster, and sure enough their worst fears were confirmed. For the poster bore the same decorative logo, but in even bigger bold black font at the top of the poster, the word, or the acronym, **F.A.R.T.**, was emblazoned onto it.

'Well', said Archie a little taken aback. 'I originally said it should be known as five against rotary turbines. I could have used a numeral and the letters A.R.T., but you wanted it to be folk. And I was right, cause there are five of us now, you, me, Rhea, Willie and Calum, as Jean and Murdoch are out of action. Anyhow', he added defensively, 'at least it'll stick in people's minds'.

'Oh, it'll certainly do that, Archie', said John acerbically. 'It'll certainly do that'.

John gave the poster back to Willie and started to walk up the road towards the Council chamber.

'Great', he said to Rhea, 'we're going to be known forevermore as the fart protest'.

As he and Rhea walked up to the Council chamber as part of the big procession, walking past the boarded up shops with their iron shutters and graffiti, reminded him of why this was just so important. In the end of the day, it didn't matter what was on the badges, or the posters, what was important was ensuring that the Council considered the facts and the devastating impact this proposed wind farm development would have on the island.

He and Rhea discussed together the main points they wanted to get across at both the Council meeting, and in any interviews with the media that might take place during, or after, it.

John asserted the importance he attached to being very factual in the Council hearing, whereas they agreed Rhea could be more emotive in her arguments to try and ensure there was an increased public awareness and support for their campaign.

As he reached the glass doorway which served as the main entrance to the Council Offices and the Council chamber, he thought to himself whether or not he should address the crowd. However, it was very noisy, and much to his chagrin, someone had started chanting, *"What Do We Want?"* with the response, *"To Break Wind. When do we want to? Now"*. As a catchphrase it had seemed to have caughtened on and proved to be one which others were only too keen to pick up on and join in reciting. Instead, he raised his fist in the air as he walked through the door, to an accompanying cheer.

At least it's stopped them from shouting that, he thought to himself.

Approaching the Reception desk, he explained he was here to speak at the Council's Planning meeting, and was taken through to a waiting room, where he was able to make himself some tea.

Across the room from him sat a man who looked very dapper in his suit and tie. He was drinking coffee, was on his mobile phone and had a briefcase down by his side.
John thought that perhaps he must be another Councillor.

Brian Whittington sat on the opposite side of the room, and looked at the slightly elderly man, as he was brought through by the receptionist to the waiting room.

He was dressed smartly and got himself some tea from the machine on the table.
It was when he went to take his seat, that Brian noticed he was wearing a badge with what he thought was the symbol of a wind turbine on it. This must be the opposition, he thought to himself.

John pulled out his notes which he'd placed in the folder with the petition in it, which Calum had handed to him at the pier, and started to read them over in his head. Brian watched on, trying to sense if the man looked anxious, but he never got that feeling.
In fact, he was concerned that he was watching someone who seemed intent on being prepared and focused on what he was doing. This certainly didn't seem to be someone from the tin hat brigade, whose viewpoints he was usually able to ridicule to Councillors.

No, this was someone who seemed to mean business, and that was not really what he wanted to see at this stage in proceedings.

As John looked up from his notes thoughtfully, he was conscious he was being watched from the other side of the room.
Just then, the Clerk to the Committee appeared from the Council Chamber, and came over first to the man across the room, and then to himself, and invited both into the Council chamber.

Just at that point another man appeared slightly out of breath, whom John recognised. He was from the neighbouring village of Clachan. He was glad to have someone else from the island at the meeting who had obviously felt strongly enough to come and make a personal representation to the Committee.

Having been a Union Steward, John was used to presenting cases at disciplinary hearings in front of two, sometimes three people, but as he entered the Chamber and looked around, he realised that this was a very different set-up altogether.

Around the room, behind microphones sat twelve men.

In the middle of a semi-circle of chairs and desks in front of them, sat the Clerk, who had shown them in.

To the side of the men behind the microphones, sat another man.

The Chairperson of the Planning Committee opened the meeting by welcoming everyone, and advised that they had reached the part of the meeting, where they were to listen to the arguments for and against the Planning application, to develop a windfarm with six wind turbines on Glen Bria, on the Dark Isle. He outlined, that the Planning Officer, in this instance the Chief Planning Officer for the Council, had compiled a report which he would talk to and then they would question him on it. After that, they would call on Arthur Smith from the village of Clachan, on the Dark Isle, to speak, before asking John to do so on behalf of the action group. The Councillors could ask questions of each speaker, before the Project Development Manager for the company seeking to build the windfarm, would be called to make their closing arguments. Similarly, Councillors could ask him questions too.

The Councillor for the island would then be asked to address the Planning Committee.

They were all advised they would strictly have three minutes in which to make their cases, and that they should not speak thereafter or participate in the Council's deliberations.
A decision, they hoped, would be made later in the day and posted on the Council's website on the next working day, being Monday, before the close of business.

'I invite the Chief Planning Officer of the Council, to talk to his report', the Chairperson invited.

As he came forward to a box in which to speak, the Clerk came over and switched the microphone on for him. A little red halo around the microphone appeared to indicate he was live. As he did so, John was sure he could hear the noise of the protestors outside the chamber.

With the additional passengers from the second ferry swelling their ranks, the volume of the protest had seemed to increase.

Just as the Chief Planning Officer inside was beginning to talk to his report, outlining the detail of the proposed development with reference to page numbers in the report, Rhea was conscious that outside the building, a regional B.B.C. camera crew and reporter had appeared. She made her way over to them and introduced herself as the Campaign group's spokesperson.

It was noisy, and the reporter took her around the side of the building to talk to her as she could not hear her, with the cameraman hot on their tail.

'What I'd like to do is interview you, if that's okay?' asked the reporter, once she'd clarified who Rhea was. 'But I need to get some of the people holding placards behind you, ideally waving them around when I do so', she informed.

'That's fine', said Rhea. 'I'm sure anyone holding a placard will oblige'.

'That's great', said the reporter, 'maybe you could call a few over'. As Rhea went to move away and call on a few of the protesters, the reporter called after her.
'What shall I call you?' she shouted.

'Di, or, Rhea', Rhea shouted back.

As the Chief Planning Officer came to the end of his report, he drove a knife through John's heart, with the simple statement,
'I would recommend the Council support the proposal, and grant a licence, for a twenty five year period to the applicant'.

John was aghast.
'Support?' he cried aloud.

'Order, please', called the Chairperson. 'You will be given your chance shortly to give your view, but first I call on Arthur Brown from the village of Clachan, who wishes to talk in support of the proposed development.

'In *support?'* cried John aghast.

Brian Whittington could not help but smirk, but tried to conceal it with his hand across his mouth.

'Order please!' shouted the chairman. 'I will have to ask you to leave the chamber if these outbursts continue', he advised.

John was dismayed, but more so at Arthur Brown. He did not usually feel prejudiced about anyone on the island, but deep down it didn't come as a surprise to him, that it would be someone from Clachan who would prove to be so traitorous to the cause.

As Arthur Brown approached the box that had been vacated by the Chief Planning Officer to the Council, the Clerk to the Committee came over to ensure his microphone was working. The red halo around it came on.

'My name is Arthur Brown and I live on the Dark Isle', he opened.

Aye, for a few months in the year in your holiday home, thought John.

'I do not intend to talk for the three minutes, but I want it placed on record that I support the proposal. I think it will bring a reduction in fuel bills of around £350 a year, which we all need amidst a cost of living crisis'.

The bugger has got two homes, screamed John to himself in his head.

'I think it will bring enormous benefits to the island, which let's be honest, has been treated very badly by those who choose to live there full-time'.

Choose to live there full-time, thought John. We don't have a bloody choice but to live there full-time.

'It will bring jobs in both the construction and operational phases', Arthur continued, 'and will also, I understand from the community consultation event, bring money to the community to invest in the village hall and other amenities, which the people, let's be honest here, have let fall into a terrible state. I have nothing further to add'.

'Thank you, Mr. Brown', said the Chairperson. 'Has anyone any questions for Mr. Brown?' he asked, raising his eyebrows and looking around the room at his colleagues.

'Yes, I have one question', said the Green Councillor for one of the mainland Wards.

'Go ahead', invited the Chairperson.

'Do you know if other islanders are in support of the proposed development too?' he asked.

'Yes', he responded immediately and emphatically. 'Many people I have spoken to have said the same', he informed.

'How many?' asked the Councillor.

'Lots', he replied.

'Can you quantify that for us?' the Green Councillor asked, but the Chairperson intervened.

'Do not harangue the member of the public, please', he said. 'He has given up his time to come here this morning and give his views to the Council, and I think he has answered your question. Now, unless anyone has any further questions for Mr. Brown, I would like to take this opportunity to thank him'.

There was a short period of silence.

'You may stand down, Mr. Brown', the Chairperson concluded.

Arthur Brown rose from the seat behind the box and returned to his seat in the auditorium.

Outside the Council Building, Rhea had gathered a small group of protesters, each with their placards held aloft in the background behind her. The cameraman ensured he got the door with the Council sign and logo in his field of view too. The reporter opened, speaking into the camera.

'I'm here, live outside the Council Headquarters, where inside a controversial planning decision to site six wind turbines on the picturesque Dark Island, is being considered'.

That was a good opening, thought Rhea, feeling enthused.

The reporter continued looking at the protesters and then back towards the camera.

'Gathered outside are the unusually named, Fart protest group, who have come from the island to make the councillors, who are sitting at this moment to determine the application, aware of their concerns. I am joined here by Diarrhoea as part…'

'No!' exclaimed Rhea, then speaking very precisely yet indignantly said, 'It's Di *or* Rhea'.

The reporter began again.
'I must apologise, I'm here with Di*ARR*hoea as part of the Fart movement'.

In her earpiece, as could be picked up on the audio on the televised broadcast, the laughter from inside the studio could be heard.

'Tell me Di*ARR*hoea, why fart?' asked the reporter all too innocently.

Once again, a roar of laughter could be heard in the news studio and on screen.

'What does it hope to achieve?' she continued quickly trying to talk over it.

'That's *not my name*. It's *Di!*' Rhea hollered at her.

'I'm ever so sorry', said the reporter. 'So, tell us then Di, why fart?'

More laughter on the earpiece and on-screen could be heard.

'Why not fart?' Di shot back out of sheer frustration.

The reporter, who was getting flustered at both the continued laughter in her earpiece and the hostility of the interviewee, continued.

'Let me rephrase that for you and for the viewers at home. What benefit can a Fart movement possibly bring to try and resolve the problem here?'

In the studio there was now uproarious laughter and the news report broke away from the scene and back to the studio, where the news presenter was doing their best to keep a straight face.

Inside, John was oblivious to the commotion outside and fifty miles away, in a T.V. studio, as well as in living rooms up and down this part of the country.

'I now call on John MacDonald, to speak on behalf of Dark Isle Folk Against Rotary Turbines', the Chairperson said.

As John walked over to the speaker's box, the Clerk followed him and turned on the microphone, which was encircled by red light. He was live. He opened his folder and took out the document within, holding it aloft, and began to speak into the microphone.

'On behalf of the Dark Isle Folk Against Rotary Turbines, I have here a petition signed by islanders, which makes it clear, that we strongly oppose the proposed development, as it stands, in its current form'.

Much to John's surprise the Chairperson interrupted him, just as he was about to outline the reasons why.

'How many have signed it, Mr. MacDonald?' he asked.

'I have five hundred signatures on it', John disclosed.

'That's less than a sixth of the island's population then, isn't it'? he remarked curtly, 'but please, go on and tell us why'.

'The reasons we oppose them are three-fold. Firstly', he said, 'we strongly believe the siting of six very large and visible wind turbines across Glen Bria and into the Bria Woods, will despoil the environment of its natural beauty, for both residents on the island and for those who visit it.

Secondly, we are concerned that the trees in the ancient woodland will be felled to provide a site for the turbines, which will decimate what is a natural habitat for much of the wildlife, flora and fauna on the island. A windfarm will disturb the natural peatland, where concrete will be used to bed the turbines in place. Lighting of the turbines, due to their height, will mean the Dark Isle, will no longer be a dark sky environment. There will be no more birdlife nearby, as the rotary blades will decimate the bird population, and nesting will no longer be able to take place, where trees have been felled. Furthermore', he added, 'the local community will be torn apart on that part of the island, where the rotary turbines are to be installed, and where people have farmed their croft lands, some for decades, and some whose families were settled here centuries ago.

As islanders, many in generations past were forced from their homes and re-settled off the island, often going abroad, but in more recent times, migration from it for reasons of economics, has threatened the way of life on the island.'

'You have one minute left. Do bring your comments to a close now, please', interrupted the Chairperson.

John continued, 'That decline in the island's population, has been steadied somewhat over the last few decades, with the provision of secondary education at the school in Clachan, and also due to modern technological innovations, and the siting of this development on the island, will only serve to reverse the progress that has been made.

It's for these reasons, Mr. Chairperson, members of the Committee, that we strongly urge you to reject this proposal'.

John took a deep breath. He felt quite pleased with how it had gone, despite the interruption when in mid-flight. He had managed to get across the main points which he wanted to make, but he couldn't believe that had used up his whole time allowance. The three minutes had seemed to fly by.

Once again, the Chairperson spoke.
'Thank you. Has anyone any questions for Mr. MacDonald?' he asked, looking around the room.

One Councillor from a mainland Ward spoke first.

'You claimed in your statement, Mr. MacDonald did you not, that the natural beauty of the island would be affected by the proposal?'

'I do believe I said words to that effect', said John, unsure what the questioner was driving at.

'But if we are to consider aesthetics as being the main criteria upon which we base a planning decision, where do we draw the line with this argument?' the Councillor stated turning to his colleagues.

'Where do we draw the line?' asked John, repeating it again. 'We draw the line when it affects our living environment, Sir. We draw the line when it affects all those who live on the island and their livelihoods. But even that is a narrow argument, for it is the wildlife, much of which has been around, long before people even settled here, which occupy that environment too'.

The Chairperson interrupted.
'It was a rhetorical question, Mr. MacDonald, not an invite for you to make another speech. You have had your three minutes for that, so I am cutting off your microphone at this point', he informed.

No further questions, specific or rhetorical were raised, and the Chairperson moved on and invited Brian up to the speaker's box.

'Is there anything you would like to clarify or elucidate in relation to your application, Mr. Whittington?' the Chairperson asked.

'Thank you, Sir', he said. 'I will be brief and speak within the time allocated to me', he smiled looking over at John.

'The concerns raised are quite simply erroneous on several fronts. I would point out that rather than diminish, or restrict the lifestyle of those in the community on the island in some way, as has been claimed, the economic value that the wind farm will bring, in terms of construction and its operation, will be an economic boost to the island economy.

A boost, that will happen year on year during the lifetime of the Project, to the tune of £150,000 per annum, once it is up and running.

That is an estimated £3.75 million over the lifetime of the development.

Secondly, the Government is in the process, it has advised, of bringing forward legislation to provide additional environmental safeguards to ensure Projects such as ours, secure environmental biodiversity.

I would also point out, in conclusion', he informed, 'that the turbines are of such a height that the wind layers generated from the turbines, will be above the tree crowns.

Any tree felling impact that there might be, to enable the turbines to be transported through the woods and up the Glen, have been mitigated, as we are able to use the existing forestry track through the woods. I hope that clarifies and answers for the Committee any concerns there might be'.

After Brian had spoken, and not been given any questions to answer which he knew was a good sign, the Chairperson invited the local Councillor for the island to address the Committee.

Switching his own microphone on, he simply said, 'I have nothing more to add to the arguments put forward by Mr. MacDonald, in terms of the strongly held objections raised by the community, to the proposed development'.

'Oh, that's good. We can maybe start to move to consideration of the application then', retorted the Chairperson.

'However', the island's Councillor added, 'I am left thinking, that should the Council choose to approve the Planning application, as recommended by the Chief Planning Officer, then what do the islanders do to influence the outcome of what happens on their island, and in their local community?'

'I don't quite understand what you mean', intervened the Chairperson. 'Can you elucidate on that for us?' he asked.

'What I mean, is that if the islanders are against a proposal, whether that be the majority, or, even if all voted against it, unanimously, and this Council approved it, then what is the point in having the vote at all? If they can't influence the outcome, or have a sense that what they say will influence it, then it creates, no, we will have created a democratic deficit. That is indeed a dangerous scenario, because if people cannot influence decision-making, by democratic means, what is left open to them but extremism?'

'My friend', said the Chairperson in a derogatory tone of voice, 'You're not suggesting for a moment that the good people of the Dark Isle, will take up arms against their local Council? Or are you?' he asked.

'No, of course not', said the island's Councillor, 'but I am concerned people will feel disaffected from the electoral process, if they can no longer see any value, or point, in exercising their vote. That is not a healthy situation, for any democratic institution, or indeed for any democracy', he concluded.

'Thank you', said the Chairperson. 'I am sure our colleagues will take that into account when considering how to vote on the matter before us', he affirmed.

Following the local Councillor's input, the Clerk came over and asked the three men who were independent of the Council, and had been invited to attend and speak, to follow him out of the Chamber, where they were taken to the waiting room and advised they were free to go.

The Clerk reminded them all that the Council's decision would be posted on the website by five o'clock on the following Monday.

As John walked down the corridor, he was glad he had got his points across, but was irritated by the experience.

When he got outside, and was momentarily blinded by the light, he soon spotted Archie. Rhea was with him too.

'How did it go?' asked the big man.

'I think I got the points we wanted to make across okay. But if I'm honest, I didn't really expect it to go the way it did', he informed.

'Why not?' asked Rhea.

'I found the level of hostility from the chairperson to be maybe masking a bias on their part, if I'm honest', John explained. 'What about you?' he added. 'Did we get any publicity?'

'Oh, we got publicity alright, or at least I certainly did. I'm destined to be known forevermore, across the land, as the FART woman'.

'Yes, we really need to change that acronym, Archie', said John shaking his head.

'Well, it's certainly damn well memorable', replied the big man, still a little offended at the response to all his handiwork.

'We will find out the outcome on Monday before five o'clock', John informed.

'That's good', Rhea replied. 'By then Murdoch will be home and hopefully Jean will be feeling better too. We should all meet in the pub together to wait for the decision coming through. It might also generate a bit of business for Calum too'.

'Jean', said John aloud, having forgot about his wife's plight from earlier in the morning. 'Here, have you got your phone with you, Rhea?' he asked.

'Yes', she replied taking it from her handbag and passing it to him.

'Can I use it to phone Jean?' he asked.

'Sure, that's why I am giving you it', she replied laughing.

John hesitated for a moment.

'Eh, do you know her number?' he asked, feeling embarrassed that he didn't know it.

'Yes, it's in my contacts list', she advised, and brought the number up on the phone which called it automatically for him.

John took a few steps away and, in a few moments, began to speak into the phone. He soon joined Rhea and Archie again and had a smile on his face.

'Is she okay?' Rhea asked.

'Yes', said John with some laughter.

'What's so funny?' asked Rhea.

'It's a little embarrassing, and I shouldn't really tell you, but her stomach pain was due to constipation, and now that she's had an enema, which thank goodness worked, she can't stop breaking wind'.

It seemed to be such a fitting note on which to end the day.

A CROWDED BAR

'This is brilliant for business', exclaimed Calum, looking at the groups of people congregated together and throughout the bar.

'You can blame Rhea for that, when you see her', informed John. 'On the journey home she went round everyone on the ferry, and told them we would all be meeting at four o'clock here at the pub, to wait for the planning committee's decision'.

'And how will we get it?' asked Calum.

'They will post it on their website. Jean and Rhea, and just about everyone else I know these days, have a smartphone, so we'll soon find out what the decision is', John informed.

Jean held her phone aloft.

'Talk of the devil', said Archie, and Murdoch pushed by Rhea on a wheelchair, came through the door to the Bar.

'Murdoch, how are you?' asked John, rising to his feet.

'What can I get you both to drink?' asked Archie.

'A half and a half would be fine for me', replied Murdoch. 'Rhea?' he said.

'I'll just have a fresh orange juice and lemonade', she informed.

'So, what's the Doctor saying now?' asked John.

'Just to go easy. No twisting or lifting over the next six weeks, and to meet with the physiotherapist each week. I'll be back on my feet in no time', Murdoch assured them.

Archie returned from the bar with drinks for them.

'And you Jean', said Rhea. 'Are you feeling better now?' she asked.

'Oh, much, thank you. Though I don't know if I have quite got over the fact that John told you all about my little problem', she said glowering at him.

'Don't worry about that', consoled Rhea. 'At least you weren't the laughing stock of the country. I'll be the one who's forever known as having the flatulence issues'.

They all laughed. Rhea started to play on her mobile phone.

'Talking of which', said John trying to deflect the ire of his wife's stare. 'Archie, have you changed the design of the badges and posters?' he asked.

'I have that, and I've brought one of the badges to show you. What I did was go round everyone on the ferry home, and ask them if they would hand them back in so I could adjust them'.

'Oh, that was very conscientious of you', remarked Rhea, looking up from the phone in her hand.

'So, here is the new version', informed Archie, pulling it from his pocket. 'You said you introduced yourself as the Dark Isle Folk Against Rotary Turbines at the Council meeting'.

'I was introduced as that by the Chairperson', John corrected, 'so I adopted it myself'.

'Exactly, so I've adjusted the badges accordingly', informed Archie, proudly presenting it and putting it on the middle of the table for them all to have a look at.

'What have you changed exactly?' asked John a little confused.

'The name', said Archie, a little put out that his friend had not noticed.

'I don't believe it', exclaimed Rhea looking up from her screen to admire the new design. 'You've done it again, Archie'.

'What?' said Archie, unsure of what she was meaning.

'I'm still going to be known as the fart woman. It's now even personalised!' she bellowed.

It was true enough, the badge retained the same design. On the dark blue background with white ripples to demarcate waves, was the big wind turbine with its propellers, right in the middle of an island on which it stood. Around the edge of the badge, he had changed the letters to read in big bold print,

Di F.A.R.T.'s

'That's my *real* name', she added. 'Maybe if you'd used all Capital letters it *might* not have been so bad, but it clearly says Di'.

'But I had to squeeze the additional letters in', he said. 'There just wasn't the room, so I had to make the I for island, a small letter', explained Archie. 'Anyway, that took me quite a few hours as I had two hundred to change'.

'Two hundred!' exclaimed John.

'Yes', said Archie feeling really defensive. 'These cost me about £40 to make, you know', he added.

'I don't suppose it matters much now anyway', John replied. 'The march is over and I don't foresee another one'.

'What if they approve the application, what will we do then dear?' asked Jean.

'They can't ignore the widespread opinion across the island', John reasoned, but inside he was not so sure.

'No decision has been posted yet', informed Rhea, 'but I'll keep checking'.

'Well, if there's nothing up on their website before five, we will still hear the outcome, as the Councillor is due off the ferry shortly and agreed to meet us here', John advised.

'That'll be really helpful', Murdoch proposed, 'as he can advise us how best to respond should they come forward with a modified proposal'.

'A modified proposal?' asked Jean.

'Yes, often these Projects will amend their proposal to take account of local concerns, but it usually amounts to something similar. It's much harder for the Council to refuse it, if they have shown they have taken account of public opinion', Murdoch outlined.

'Oh, I see', said Jean.

'Well, they are not going to have to do that', informed Rhea.

'What do you mean?' asked John.

'It's up', she said standing to her feet.
'Listen up!' she shouted to everyone in the bar but the noise was too much to be heard.

Calum noticing she was trying to get everyone's attention bellowed.

'Order. Let's listen to what Rhea has got to say!'

The room silenced. She stood on her stool.

'The Council's Planning Committee have posted their decision on the Council's website. They have *approved* the wind farm application', she said aloud, the distaste which she felt for the decision being apparent in her expression.

There was much noise and consternation in the pub at her devastating announcement.

'I don't bloody believe it', said Murdoch stunned by the outcome.

'They just can't do that' said Jean quietly.

'They can, love, and they have', said John mournfully. 'Maybe if I had been more forceful at the meeting, or had put forward a better argument, it might have been different'.

'Rubbish', said Archie, who was not usually one for being vocal. 'There is no-one I know who can put an argument across on behalf of other people, as well as yourself, John', he countered.

John put his hand on Archie's shoulder in acknowledgement of his support.

'Absolutely right', remarked Murdoch. 'Indeed, there is no finer. But for all that, we must now focus on what steps we should take next'.

At this point the pub went silent, as the Councillor for the island walked through the door. But the silence was shortlived, and everyone started booing.

'Would you shut up everyone, and let the man speak', bellowed Calum from behind the bar. An eerie silence descended upon the room.

'I see that you have all heard the decision of the Planning Committee. For that I am sorry', he gulped. 'Please don't shoot the messenger. I did vote against it. There were ten votes for the application; one against, that being me; and one abstention', he informed.

John got to his feet and came over to the Councillor, offering to buy him a drink, in solidarity, but also to try and show people that the Councillor was not the enemy in this case.

That seemed to help defuse things, as everyone went back to their own personal discussions in their groups. John led the Councillor to the table, around which the five of them were seated.

'I'm utterly appalled and ashamed', said Jean, who was also not one for speaking out much. 'How can they ignore the wishes of all the people on the island?'

'That is exactly the point I made at the Council meeting, which your husband was at', informed the Councillor.

'So, how do we appeal the decision?' asked Murdoch.

'Clearly the developer is just trying to make money', added Rhea.

'Yes, that is undoubtedly true', the Councillor replied, 'but the motive of any applicant is not a reason that the Council will take into account in any planning application'.

'But given the number of turbines', Murdoch interjected, 'clearly the electricity produced far exceeds the island's need, so the intention is to export the surplus off the island, which will require further infrastructure and development'.

'I agree', he responded, 'but once again a suspicion that further development would be required, is not something the Council is allowed to take into consideration in determining an application'.

'Aye, but they can fail to take into account the islanders' wishes', Archie retorted sharply.

'Look, I know you are upset', said the Councillor. 'I'm upset too. My family have lived on the north end of the island for fifty five years now'.

'So, how do we appeal the decision?' asked Murdoch, always the pragmatist. 'Can we appeal to the Secretary of State?'

'Unfortunately not', the Councillor said shaking his head. 'Only the applicant can appeal to the Secretary of State. The only route for anyone who objects to the decision is a legal one, and that has to be on the basis that the correct procedures were not followed. I think there is also a time limit of six weeks on raising any action of this nature with the courts'.

'Courts', said Murdoch. 'That would be quite a hefty expense'.

'We could crowd fund it', said Rhea. 'If everyone on the island gave, say a fiver, that would give us fifteen thousand pounds, and some people would give us more, surely'.

'You've got to remember', suggested Murdoch, 'that there are quite a few children in that number, and although there are few, there will also be some who support the application. What about our representative in Parliament?' he thought aloud. 'Could they not pressurise the Government to call the application in?'

'Look', said the Councillor, knocking back the rest of his whisky. 'I need to get home as my wife hasn't seen me since last week. If you want my opinion, don't waste your time fundraising. The Council, as much as I abhor the decision made, have followed the procedures. There are no grounds for an appeal. As for the Government, I hate to burst your bubble, but the Wind Farm will be right up their street as it will help them reach their net zero target'.

With these parting comments he stood up, bid his hosts farewell, and exited the pub quickly lest anyone stop him enroute.

'Well, I'll stop them,' said Archie.

'Admirable, Archie', said John, 'but how do you propose to do that?'

'They'll have to get round me first', he exclaimed. 'Why don't you try?' he jested.

'Ha!' replied John. 'I would never even attempt such a thing'.

They all laughed.

'But maybe Archie has a point', countered Murdoch. 'Maybe we can still protest and show our objection to the development, and generate greater public awareness and support against it, on both the island and the mainland'.

'Without the badges', shot Rhea.

'Ok, without the badges. But it's got to be civil disobedience', Archie retorted.

'Up to a point,' said Murdoch. 'Up to a point'.

'What do you have in mind?' asked John and a lengthy and slightly hushed conversation ensued amongst them.

TIMBER

It was with some surprise, that work on developing the site for the windfarm followed on so quickly from the Planning Committee's decision to approve it, and grant it a licence.

The ferry had to do two separate runs exclusively for the lorries with their long trailers, which were to be stationed on the island, presumably for carrying the turbines to their final destination up the Glen.
This proved quite a challenge for the ferry, given the ship's length was just over 40 metres, and each trailer was 55 metres. Fortunately, the trailers for carrying the turbines were designed in such a way as to close into a more compact size of 22 metres, so they managed to fit on the empty car deck.

In the woods at Glen Bria, shortly after sunrise, on one Spring morning, the sound of mechanical circular saws could be heard.
It drowned out the sound of the running water from the nearby river, as the track which ran the length of the woods was being widened, by removing some of the trees.

Some of the old wooden posts were also removed, to ensure the lorries would be able to get up the Glen with their intended loads. Each lorry could carry up to 40 tonnes in weight.

The horses in the nearby field were *neighing*, passing comment on the disturbance the workmen were causing.

Up near the entrance to the Glen, by the six monoliths, the woodsmen had felled quite a few trees, to provide a turning circle for the long vehicles that would have to make a turn at this point, and head up the more open Glen itself.

Archie watched on from a distance, having walked from the entrance to the Shee Gate. Walking a little further along the track, he veered off into the woods and away from where the work was being done. He knew the woods like the back of his hand, having played here through the years as a child. To the children of Bria village, it had been a natural Adventure Playground for them.

After a while walking through the woods, he cut down between the trees and rejoined the main track, near to the Clachan Gate.

What he saw, was more intensive tree felling beyond that gate.

The Forestry workers were felling the trees, which in fairness was what the Sitka spruce and pine plantation was intended for, but on this occasion, it was to ensure there was a clear access to and from the nearby coastal road.

Over the next few weeks, an additional bit of forestry track was to be laid to circumvent the need for going under the old road bridge, which was far too narrow for the lorries, which would carry the components of the wind turbines to site.

Brian Whittington stood at the entrance to the Clachan Gate with his helmet on, and looked down towards where the intended track would be sited, then up the hill where additional surfacing would be undertaken to widen it.

He turned to the foreman and gave a few directions, before a smile of satisfaction grew across his face.

Later that evening in the pub, where he had been joined by Murdoch and Rhea, Jean and John, Archie had made a declaration.

'When the propellers come, I'll drag them off and hide them'.

Murdoch laughed.
'I know you are built like an Ox, Archie', he said, 'but even you would struggle trying to pull a 16 tonne weight behind you. And anyway, where would you hide them?'

'I'd dig a trench and hide them all', he said in a very serious tone of voice.

'I see just north of the pier', John informed, 'they have started work to build the new marine port for delivering the turbines. They have laid a large concrete base, and in the water are all these floating modular pontoons, enabling the workmen to work alongside it, reinforcing the bank, from the water's edge. Ironically', he observed, 'I don't think there is one local workman among them'.

Despite Archie's restlessness and feelings of militancy, they cautioned him to stick to the plan.

D-DAY

Over the next fortnight, and impatient and powerless to stop things as they all increasingly felt, the creeping industrialisation of the island continued apace.

John felt that the landing bay at the new marine port, was sadly a fitting addition to the carbuncle of a pier and gangway, which they had built to replace the old pier several years ago. He had described it as being like an aircraft hangar at the time. A brutal concrete ramp at the end of the pier road, with the enormous skeletal like crane sitting upon it, only seemed now to add to that overall impression.

Rhea had spent some of her time contacting the local radio station, and had secured for herself an interview slot, which she felt for once had enabled her to get the salient points across that had been overlooked in her television interview, when the name of the campaign group had commandeered the spotlight.

Murdoch was feeling very frustrated. Being largely confined to the wheelchair, he could not get around and observe the work that was going on, without getting someone to wheel him there.

The woods were also a no-go area while the work was going on to fell some of the trees, widen, reinforce and build new track, for the future transportation of the components of the wind turbines to the proposed site.

Feeling that his independence had been greatly curtailed, he set about doing what Murdoch did best, and that was learning about the ins and outs of what was being constructed.

So, he busied himself with research at his computer. He was perturbed that the development had a capacity of 30 Megawatts, far in excess of what was needed for the island. Further research which he undertook, also revealed that the windfarm company, was in fact a front for a multinational parent company. This parent company which provided services globally across the world, needed the ability to generate electricity to power its data centres. Murdoch suspected the windfarm on the Dark Isle, was part of a much bigger plan, to set up a network of wind farms, with a view to constructing and powering a data centre. The Dark Isle was just another resource to be exploited to that end.

Jean, also did what Jean did best, which was to run about trying to help everyone in whatever way she could with campaign work.

She had been more than happy to drive Murdoch down the pier, so he could see all the work that was going on, which John had described.

She was quite content to type letters for John which he sent off to the local and national press. Technology had never been his strong point, with much of his written work being drafted out in a small blue notebook which he kept with him.

She was even happy to sit with Archie, and help him make up new badges with the same logo surrounded by the words in bold print,

No Turbines

Calum, who had got more involved in the day to day working of the campaign, as well as doing his pub work, started to utilise one of his underused skills.

Although he presented as a happy go lucky man whose sole purpose and pleasure in life was being a bartender, he had in fact when he was younger, performed well academically in his school years, and had gone to University.

The island had its share of really clever people, often with extensive experience in many fields, who for whatever reason of their own, had given up that way of life and were now living a quiet life in retirement on the island, or were performing a wholly different role, like waiter, or cleaner in a hotel, or in Calum's case, bartender.

When at University, he had taken a degree in physics and meteorology and was, with the correct tools, quite capable of turning out a local weather forecast based upon the current localised weather patterns. He had for several years run a local forecasting service on the internet. He still had all his equipment set up in the beer garden, in fact, it housed the only thing to resemble a wind turbine on the island up to that point, as he had an anemometer for measuring wind speed. Given what was being planned, he thought now was the time to resurrect it, albeit privately.

It was no secret that at some point in the next month or two, the company who were building the windfarm would be delivering the components of the wind turbines.
Normally, these are simply transferred by road.

On an island, there were different considerations being surrounded by water. Initially, the intention was that these would arrive by barge, which would dock at the marine port. From there the nacelle, the turbine which generates the power, the tower sections, and the rotor blades and hub, would be loaded on to the concrete platform which had been built for that purpose.

The lorries that had come onto the island, would then meet them, and would transport the parts from the north pier, to the site in Glen Bria.

As the Campaign group had learned, there was much secrecy about the date and time that was proposed for delivery.

Murdoch had thought about submitting a Freedom of Information request to discover this. Indeed he had done so, but given the company was a private concern, they simply passed it to the Local Council. Regardless, they had twenty days in which to respond and delivery could happen at anytime, day or night.

So, Murdoch had had the brainwave of asking the Harbourmaster, what the proposed date of delivery was. He had responsibility for securing the service of Pilots and their vessels, which would be used to bring such a large vessel to the marine port.

In response, he was curtly told that this was commercially sensitive information, which he could not disclose.

This is where Archie came into his own.

Having been born and bred on the island, there was no-one whom Archie did not know.

It wasn't so much his stature which encouraged people to help, or respond to him, with any requests he might have. It was quite the reverse, in that his gentle nature helped him make inroads where others could not.

When Murdoch suggested to Archie that he might be best placed to secure the information that the campaign group was seeking, Archie was unsure he could do so.

The Harbourmaster, as much as he was a decent enough fellow, was not local to the island. He and his family had come about ten years ago to it. But then Archie had a brain wave.

Archie was good friends with 'Wille the Fish', as he was known. He was called 'Wille the Fish', either to distinguish himself from another tradesman, 'Willie the Joiner', who was known on the island. He had helped make the placards for the protest march. The alternative explanation was that he was given the name simply because he was the only trawlerman left on the island.

The island used to support twelve trawlers, but between overfishing, quota restrictions and other economic factors, Wille was the only fisherman left on the island. There was also 'Lobby the Lobster', who had his own single person creel boat, but Willie was your traditional fisherman with a trawler.

Archie knew Wille the Fish had a good relationship with the Harbourmaster, so he asked him straight out one night at the pub, if he could find out from him the date and time of the delivery of the turbines.

So, Willie bribed the Harbourmaster, a north eastern man, with a personal week's supply of Cod, and the information that was much needed was revealed.

Delivery Day would be the following Monday at six o'clock in the morning.

SAILING CLOSE TO THE WIND

'I don't like it', cautioned Calum looking at his created weather charts. 'There is a deep low moving in bringing strong easterlies over the Sound'.

'And what does that mean?' asked John verbalising his frustration.

'It means, it's going to be quite stormy, for 24 hours I would say. But then, you will have a period of calm', Calum informed.

'What sort of windspeed are you talking about?' asked Murdoch.

'As an estimate, 35 miles an hour, or Force 7 as they say on the Beaufort Scale', Calum advised.

'But that's not going to stop a barge that size, surely?' interrupted Archie.

'No, that's true', said Calum patiently, 'But it's going to stop you'.

'I don't reckon the tug boats will want to risk it', said Wille the Fish from a more informed perspective. 'The easterly wind will create a swell at the marine port, and what mariner wants to be unloading on a choppy sea. It's bad enough unloading fish boxes in those sorts of conditions, let alone wind turbines'.

'Aye, right enough', said Archie.

'No, I think guys', said Calum, 'that they will go for the next morning when it will be perfectly calm'.

'Well, Tuesday morning it is then', suggested John, and all were in agreement.

On the Sunday night, Calum waited up and listened to the shipping forecast which he rarely did. He was worried in case he might have got the forecast wrong.

Murdoch shared a similar anxiety, and was listening to the same broadcast.

Calum did get it wrong, but fortunately he got it wrong in the right way.
The forecast was in fact much worse than he'd predicted. He had been right that a deep low was heading towards the country, but it would actually produce gale force winds.

Not bad, thought Calum, considering I don't have the benefit of satellites.

John was also down at the Harbour, just after half past four on the Monday morning. At that time, the first indication of twilight was just beginning to make its presence known.
He stood at the pier and looked north.
There was no sign of any shipping movements, so equally relieved, he returned home.

It had been agreed amongst the Campaign group and all who were going to participate, that they would meet at around three the following morning.

All their planning revolved around the movements of the three Policemen on the island.

As one of the special Constables on the island had told Archie, under a promise of confidentiality, with the island only having the services of three Policemen and a few Special Constables to cover shifts, there were never any Police on duty on the island between two and six in the morning.

In addition, everyone knew that at ten o'clock each night, the Police would finish their drive through Bria village before returning to their office at Clachan. It was decided that once the road was clear, some of the crofters would drive their tractors to Bria.

On the Monday night, at the tail end of the storm, all went exactly to plan. Towing behind a convoy of tractors, were rowing boats, with which they normally fished in the fresh water lochans on the island. The crofters dropped them off by the jetty on the beach.

Other protesters, who had Kayaks, could be seen carrying their Kayaks through the village, heading down towards the shoreline by the jetty, just after half past two the next morning.

John and Archie were already down on the beach with a few of the protesters, waiting for a phone call from Willie the Fish, who would give the signal to begin, for the flotilla to put out to sea, and congregate around the marine port. Willie knew that he would not raise any suspicions whatsoever being at the harbour around three that morning. It was not an uncommon sight for he and his crew to be preparing the vessel for sea and an early morning departure.
Lobby the Lobster had also agreed to take his creel boat out too that morning.

It was now past three in the morning.

More and more protestors joined them on shore. John was getting twitchy. He could see lights out in the bay, and wondered if that might be the first signs of the barge approaching, from further north up the Firth.

'I don't know why he's not phoning', said John to Archie, getting more and more restless.

Sensing the irritation in his voice, Archie tried to reassure him that Willie would be waiting for the tide to be favourable.

'It's as still as glass out there', John had retorted. 'He better not wait too long', he added feeling increasingly agitated. 'Look at all these lights. That must be the barge and the tug boats', he reasoned aloud. 'It'll take us a good twenty minutes or so to get everyone into position'.

Just then a beam of light accompanied by a rumbling sound, much closer to them, was seen to lighten up the Bay, just where it was intended that they would start to congregate with the variety of vessels they had at their disposal.

It was then he felt the vibration in his pocket. It was Jean's phone, on which he had turned the volume off, in case the noise might alert anyone to their presence at such an unusual time of day.

'Hi, Willie', he replied to the caller. '*What?*' he said, sounding alarmed. 'Navy? Oh *for God's sake*', he cursed at the phone and started to pace up and down the beach. 'And how long will that take?' he asked clearly agitated.

By then Calum and Mike came over to join them, sensing that something was amiss.

'What's up?' asked Calum. 'Why the delay? My forecast said it would be calm come the morning, and it is'.

'Your weather forecast was spot on Calum. The problem is, Willie has just called, to say the navy submarines and a helicopter are passing through at the moment as part of an exercise'.

'How long will that take?' asked Archie.

'That's what I asked', said John. 'Willie said we should hold tight and he'll phone again when he thinks it's clear. As a fishing vessel' he says, 'he gets information on the submarines and their movements through the Firth and the Sound'.

'We've probably only got about another hour until astronomical twilight', Calum informed.

'If they don't bloody hurry up', said John, 'they'll see us and we'll lose any of the surprise element which we've got on our side'.

It was a further twenty minutes before the phone buzzed again. John turned away from the crowd and took the call. All stood silent, waiting for and hanging on his every word. It was not long before he turned to face them.

'Right, we're on!' he cried, and the boats were pushed out into the sea.
One of Archie's cousins, known as 'Big Malkie', took both John and Archie aboard.
In the distance they could also see the Sweet Mary, which was Willie the Fish's trawler and the small creel boat belonging to Lobbie, leaving the confines of the harbour.

The trawler also provided some light on the water, but fortunately not as much as had the helicopter, which had passed through the Sound earlier.

They rowed out into the open water, and headed towards where the new marine port, the slipway and landing platform had been built, and which were situated to the north of the existing pier. The flotilla of about eight rowing boats, were accompanied by about six Kayaks. The creel boat and the trawler were now already at the designated area, and they set themselves at the centre of the formation, and waited as everyone took up positions north and south of them, bobbing up and down gently on the water.

It was cold out on the water as twilight came.

The lights of the Barge approaching from north had now entered the Sound and was coming towards them.

Big Malkie had brought a flask of hot tea which they shared, and watched as the large vessel drew nearer and nearer, guided by two tug boats, one at the front and one at the rear.

As a vessel in its own right, and now at an increasingly shorter distance from them, the Barge with all its cargo loaded onboard, completely dwarfed the trawler and the creel boat. The rowing boats and Kayaks, being no more than a pin prick, on a deep blue fabric.

'It's getting a bit too close for my liking', said Malkie.

'Naw, it'll stop when they see the fishing boat', reasoned Archie, but Malkie was not so sure.

'I don't know, Archie', he said getting more and more panicked. 'These crafts are just so large, they can't just stop quickly. It does seem to be getting very close to us'.

He started nervously rummaging about under a cover on the boat, and producing a gun, shot a red flare up into the sky, lighting up the surface of the sea below it.
They could also see breaking formation was the Sweet Mary.

'*Mother of God!*' someone shouted from one of the other vessels, and some of the Kayakers, largely due to the waves being generated by the ginormous barge, started to paddle away with great difficulty from their positions.

'What's going on?' exclaimed John, confused as to why the trawler was leaving without telling them. 'Try and hold position', he shouted, but it was in vain. His cry was drowned out by five short blasts on a deafening horn, which came from the barge.

The Creel boat had also started to move away, and Willie could be seen on the deck of the Sweet Mary, waving his arms wildly back towards the direction of the rowing boats.

'I think he wants us to move away', said Big Malkie.

'But we're going to break our formation and let the barge get in if we do that', cried John.

Malkie was about to tell him that the formation was already well and truly broken, when they became conscious that to their rear, was yet another vessel approaching them. It appeared to be a small navy ship.

'Oh, oh,' said Big Malkie. 'Looks like we've got company', he said rowing powerfully away from it and towards the shore.

At this point, a voice from a loudspeaker boomed out across the sea.

'This is His Majesty's Fisheries Protection Vessel. You are instructed to move your vessels and return to shore'.

This was repeated three times.

As they approached the shore, they caught site of two vehicles, a Police Landrover and the Coastguard's van. On the beach at the end of the jetty, stood Sergeant McColl with the Coastguard in his blue woollen jersey. Wearing his uniform, the burly Policeman also wore a rather grim expression across his face.

John and Archie disembarked the rowing boat, and as they walked back up the jetty towards dry land, they were met at the end of it by the Sergeant, who was clearly very unamused.

'I've just had to get out of my bed well before my shift starts, to come down here. What do you think you are doing exactly?' he asked.

'We're operating a blockade, to prevent the barge from delivering the wind turbines to the island', John informed in a calm and factual way.

Sergeant McColl looked up at Archie, and instead focused his glare and ire upon John.

'What you are doing as far as the law is concerned, is sailing close to the wind. You are preventing the free movement of the ship on the open sea from conducting its lawful business', he informed.

'And you should not be firing flares needlessly', interrupted the Coastguard. 'That is an improper use of a flare'.

'It was hardly improper', said John rather indignantly. 'That barge was about to plough into us', he said.

'Enough', said the Policeman. 'I am arresting you on suspicion of terrorism under section 41 of the Terrorism Act 2000', he informed. 'You do not have to say anything. But it may harm your defence if you do not mention when questioned something that you later rely on in Court. Anything you do say may be given in evidence. Do you understand?'

'Terrorism!' exclaimed John.

'Aye, terrorism', said the burly Policeman. 'You understand that then', he surmised.

Archie took one step closer to the Policeman and the Coastguard, and looked as if he was about to physically intervene, so much so, the Coastguard took a step back at his presence.

The Policeman held his ground.
'Step away, Sir', he said, 'or you'll be joining him'.

Archie gave it some momentary consideration and thought better of it, heeding the Policeman's advice.
Instead, he watched on as John was led away, where he was put into the back of the Police Landrover.

Being left standing with Archie, the Coastguard decided not to press the issue of the flare any further and walked back to his vehicle. There he watched to ensure all of the flotilla had returned safely to shore.

REASSEMBLING

Although he was not himself local to the island, Sergeant McColl was related to Mike the shopkeeper in Bria village. His sister had married the policeman when he was first sent to the island many years ago, when the numbers of the Police are increased during the holiday season.

They tended to swell the ranks with policemen and policewomen, who were still on, or just coming to the end of their probationary periods, as rural policing on an island was seen as good experience to have under your belt.

Constable McColl, as he was known then, had just finished his two years' probation, when he was sent to the island over the summer months, when the population increased ten-fold, given it was a picturesque island with many holiday homes, guest houses and hotels. They even provided an additional ferry during the summer to accommodate the increased number of tourists.

Mike had managed to have a word in the big Policeman's ear, for although the shopkeeper was now part of the campaign, he was unable to participate in the blockade of the marine port and landing bay, as he had no-one to cover the shop which he had to get ready for opening later that morning.

He had heard what had happened pretty quickly however, as the shop was a hub for all the local gossip and news that went on in the island. Making a phone call to his brother-in-law, he had pointed out that intense as John was about things, his heart was in the right place as far as the island was concerned.

This had seemed to appease the agent of law enforcement on the island, as he felt it would be counter-productive to alienate a resident population on the island that was so clearly opposed to the wind farm, as he relied on their goodwill to effectively police the place.

So, it was mid-morning when John returned home, much to Jean's relief. She had only had a few hours of anxiety to control, when Archie had come by the house to tell her what had happened. The Police Sergeant had even dropped John off at home, giving him a ride in his own car, back down the hill from Clachan to Bria, at what John felt was possibly an excessive speed.

'I think you need to take a step back now, John', his wife suggested strongly.

'I can't do that', said John adamant in his response.

'The windfarm is going to go ahead, whether we like it or not', said Jean. 'And even if you think you can stop it, let someone else take the lead on it for a while', she said, resigned to the fact he would continue to the bitter end, regardless of any protest she made to the contrary.

Over the course of the next week, John did lie low, more out of fatigue than having lost his zest for the cause.

In that time, the components of the wind turbines were delivered each day, by two lorries, to the site. It was a slow process requiring police escort, certainly at a much slower pace than that at which the Sergeant had returned his prisoner during the early part of the week, back to his home.

It took six days to transport the hub, each tower section, the nacelle and each of the lengthy blades to the site at Glen Bria. Both lorries worked nine hours per day, with a break after four and a half hours, to take all of the constituent parts of the turbines to their resting place. At the beginning of the following week, each was due to be assembled.

At the end of the week, and looking to relax, John agreed to go down the pub with Archie on the Saturday night. Jean declined on this occasion, as she did not want her husband to feel that she was in any way encouraging him to reassemble the campaign group, by being present.

Regardless of her worst fears, that is exactly what ended up happening, not by design but by chance.

In the run up to the attempted blockade, the movements of the turbine parts by sea had been a closely guarded commercial secret, only broken by the promise of *'some fash'*, as the Harbourmaster discreetly named his price, in his north eastern accent.

Following the failed blockade, the flow of information about the windfarm became even more restricted.

Clearly people could see the transportation through the island, from the landing bay to the Glen, of the constituent parts of the turbines, but as to when they were due to be assembled, erected and made functional, nobody knew. That was until Calum got one of the drivers drunk one night, following his long shift of driving at a snail's pace all day.

From the driver, he had learned that the beginning of the following week, was when the turbines were due to be assembled.

'We could block the entrance', the bartender had suggested.

'I think after last week's attempt at the harbour, they will be prepared for that sort of thing', Murdoch suggested.

'We need some form of element of surprise, if it is to be effective', said John reluctantly being drawn into the plan. 'And we need to make sure there is some media presence, to raise public awareness and get people on our side. There are still people who remain unsure about it all on the island, but we need support on the mainland too'.

'Yes, John is right', agreed Murdoch. 'The planning consent and licence have been given, and all the equipment is on site. This really is the last chance saloon'.

'What if we were already *on* site, before they arrived on Monday morning?' Archie suggested.

'What, camp out?' asked John, thinking to himself the last time he had camped was probably about twenty five years ago.

'Aye, we could camp. Just go up there on the Sunday night', Archie confirmed what he was thinking.

'What about the Sabbath?' said John, a little taken aback at such a heretical notion.

'Aye, the Sabbath. Right enough', said Archie. 'Well, what about we walk up around three in the morning, and wait behind the turbine bits?'

'Aye, that would be better ', John agreed. 'There will be no Police about then, as I've become a marked man. But we can't just be standing there. We need a plan of action', said John finally losing all sense of his wife's cautionary words to him, following the previous action.

'Well, obviously in this chair I can't get up there', said Murdoch disappointed, 'but if you want, I'll try and make some contacts and see if we can get the media up there that morning'.

'Now', said Archie. 'I have an idea'.

CRUCIFIXION

It wasn't that he did not want Jean to know what was planned, but more that he did not want her to worry. So, when John sneaked out of his house on the Monday morning around half past two, he had already prepared for his flight by packing his rucksack, which he now retrieved from the garden shed.

It was years since he had last used this stuff, he thought to himself, and hoped he could remember all that he had learned.

Shutting the front door of the house as quietly as he could, he took the familiar walk up the Bria Main Road towards Archie's house. When he got there, all the houselights were on and he could hear quite a few voices. Knocking on the window, he opened the front door and was immediately overcome by music.

'Late to the party, as always!' shouted Archie, beckoning his friend inside.

Sitting around the room was Jock, the accordionist, with Duncan on the fiddle, blasting out a reel. Malkie, the crofter who had let off the flare which had got them into trouble with the Coastguard, was opening a bottle of whisky and offering Willie the Fish a drink. Calum the bartender was also being tended to, and his glass was topped up.
Archie was looking very merry and slightly the worse for wear.

'I've rounded up the gang', he said quite pleased with himself.

'Aye, right you are, Archie', said John, worried in case none of them might actually make it to the top of the Glen, or even to the entrance at the Shee Gate a hundred yards along the road. 'We need to head soon if we are going to get there before light', John suggested, 'or we will lose the element of surprise'.

'Och, have one for the road', said Malkie, getting a glass and pouring him what must have been a sextuple measure, going by Calum's rigid 25ml standard at the bar.

John resigned himself, with not too much encouragement, to having the drink. It would probably give him the courage he needed, as he was not too sure about whether or not he would be any good at executing the plan. Only time would tell.

After a few more reels and jigs, and with some of the others managing to empty the bottle which Malkie had opened when John had arrived about half an hour ago, the ceilidh came to an end. The demeanour of the men changed, as they all filed out the door. Archie almost did not make it, as uncharacteristically, he had forgotten to duck coming out of his entrance. Willie the Fish headed down to the Harbour, as he had his boat to get ready for an early morning departure.

Entering the Shee gate, they walked the distance to the Standing Stones, where the opening to the Glen was situated.

It was very muddy around that area, as although the vehicles had the benefit of a newly constructed piece of track to provide a turning circle to enable them to get up the Glen, all the work that had been done to facilitate that, had churned up the ground around the monoliths.

Worse still, as far as John and Archie were concerned, was the copse from which Murdoch had come to grief, had been felled to allow for unhindered access up the Glen, by the lorries with the long trailers bearing their heavy and lengthy loads.

Fortunately, all had appropriate footwear. Indeed, John, Archie, Malkie and Jock, had all at one time or other, been involved in the Junior Mountain Rescue Group in their youth, and both Calum and Duncan had been in the 1st Dark Isle Scouts.

That's what gave John the confidence that they might be able to pull this off.

Reaching the summit of the rolling hills, which was made considerably easier given that the track had been widened and reinforced, the six men threw down their rucksacks. The first inkling of twilight was making its appearance, and the silhouettes of the parts of the turbines, started to come into view.

Beside the site for the first turbine, they could clearly see the concrete foundation had been laid, and a plinth had been inserted within the foundation upon which to mount the turbine. The giant crane that had been at the harbour and transported to site, had been re-assembled for the building operation, and stood there towering over them. Even Archie was dwarfed by its Meccano like structure.

To the side of the plinth, lay the sections of the tower and the nacelle, which obviously they were ready to assemble, before attaching the three elongated blades.

As the neighbouring site for the second turbine came into view, it was clear it was just as well developed as the first.

'I think that changes the plan a little', said John. 'I didn't think for a moment that they were so far advanced. Clearly, this one and probably the other will be finished by the end of the day, unless we manage to stop them'.

The men unpacked some of the rucksacks and started to work.

'We need to move, or at least lift it', said John pointing to the blade. 'Where is Murdoch when you need his brains the most?' he snorted.

'I'll lift it', said Archie.

'Don't be daft, Archie!' exclaimed John. 'Have you any idea how heavy these things are?'

Archie walked to the end of the blade and at its most pointed end placed his hands behind it. He heaved and he grunted but he could not budge it an inch.

'All we need is something to give us a bit of leverage', suggested Calum. 'We could build a pulley system, but we don't have anything to turn the ropes on'.

'What about levering it up with a plank of wood?' asked Duncan.

'Not at that weight', Calum concluded. 'But look', he said pointing to one of the blades. 'You can get the rope under the end of that one, as there's a slightly bigger gap between it and the surrounding ground, compared to the other two'.

True enough, there was a small gap, and John went over, knelt down and got the rope around it.

'Who's first?' he asked.

There was a deafening silence.

'Right, I'll do it myself', he humphed. Turning to Archie, he said 'Make sure you use a re-threaded figure of eight knot around my waist, in the rare event they might actually lift the thing off the ground, with me attached to it'.

'Would that not defeat the purpose of the protest?' Calum asked with a smirk.

'Aye, it would that', said John, 'but there is no way they would risk that'.

With the remaining rope, Archie volunteered to be tied around the narrowest part of the tower section, which took Malkie and Jock all their previously learned knot tying skills to achieve, as several lengths of rope were needed to go around its diameter, and a wee bit more given Archie's diameter too.

'Well, if they are going to raise it, then I guess I'll be up first before you', Archie chuckled aloud.

The plan had been to tie each of them to the six blades. But with the Sun dawning, a lack of technical equipment to raise the blades, and the arrival of two vans, the plan had to be modified so that only Archie and John were affixed to the turbine's parts.

Calum, Jock, Duncan and Malkie, instead took positions standing blocking the entrance to the first turbine site. Much as they were ready to stand their ground, the two vans stopped short, and instead turned into the second turbine site. A few men got out the van, looked up the hill towards them, went back into their vans and just sat there.

'I wonder what they are doing?' said Archie.

They did not have to wait long for an answer, for it only took about ten minutes before the familiar Landrover, with the flashing blue light, drove up towards the two vans.

Sergeant McColl got out the Police Landrover and could be seen speaking through the window of one of the work vans to the men. Then he jumped back in his Landrover, and drove up the track to the entrance of the site of the first turbine, which was blocked by the four men.

Getting out the Landrover, he walked over to them.
'You can't block the entrance lads', he said quite calmly.

'You can't say we are obstructing the highway', replied Calum, who momentarily forgot his degree was in meteorology and physics and not law.

'No, I'm not saying that', said the burly Policeman, 'but alternatively I just arrest you for breach of the peace. How will that do instead?'

The four men stepped aside and the Sergeant walked up to where Archie was tied to the tower section. That was kind of easy, he said to himself, let's hope this ends the same way. He walked over to where John was lying on the ground, bound to the propeller.

'Oh, it's you again', he remarked.

'I'm not a terrorist, let me make that perfectly clear to you', remarked John indignantly.

'I'm asking you politely to get off that thing, Mr. MacDonald', he replied.

'No, I will not be moved', insisted John.

'Well, you are creating a breach of the peace', the Police Sergeant responded.

'Whose peace am I breaching?' John shot back at him.

'It doesn't quite mean literally', the Sergeant informed. 'You are preventing these people down the road there, from conducting their lawful business by interfering with their property'.

'Well, they are destroying the environment and interfering with countless people's livelihoods across the island', John retorted.

'Look', said Sergeant McColl, trying to sound reasonable. 'I don't disagree with your sentiments. Clearly you feel strongly about it, but you and your big chum here, are the only ones who are going to come off the worst today because of it'.

'That maybe so', said John, 'but I'm staying put'.

'And I'll follow you to the end of the earth!' cried Archie.

At this point another van could be seen coming up the track. It had a satellite dish on its roof and clearly was a television crew. The Sergeant turned around to look at it.

'Oh, by Jesus', the Policeman remarked, 'just my luck today to get Bonnie and Clyde'. Withdrawing from the turbine's parts, he walked back to his Landrover, jumped inside and began to use the radio.

True enough, it was a local television crew. In fact, it was the very same reporter who had interviewed Rhea, outside the Council chamber. Also, walking up the track, and now only coming into view, were about two dozen other protestors, whom Murdoch had rallied to give a backdrop for the camera crew for when they started to film, and hopefully interview people.

Murdoch was present and was being pushed in his wheelchair by Willie the Joiner.

As they approached the site of the first turbine, the camera crew did in fact start filming their march.

The reporter went over to Archie, and was soon followed by the camera crew.

'Speak with John over there', he suggested, motioning towards John with his head. The reporter walked over to where the massive propeller lay on the ground with John attached.

Establishing John's name from him, she began her report.

'Here I am in Glen Bria, at the site of the Windfarm which is in the process of being constructed, in the face of local opposition. I am joined by John MacDonald, one of the protesters, who is tied to a propeller'.

John didn't know if he was meant to smile, or what was appropriate in this sort of situation, so he kept a serious visage.

'Mr. MacDonald', the reporter said. 'It's rather symbolic, is it not, that you are lying in a cruciform shape, with your arms outstretched'.

'That's blasphemous', he began, but quickly changed tact. 'But it's symbolic, because the island is being crucified'.

'Why do you say that?' she asked.

'The way of life of the islanders is being crucified by this project. The crofting community is being crucified, and the woods and the local environment are being crucified at the hands of those who seek to make a profit'.

'But it is true, is it not', she asked, 'that there will be an economic boost to the island, through a community regeneration fund, set up by the energy company? The company say they are keen to work alongside the islanders'.

'It's funny', said John. 'how the islander is always expendable when there is money to be made from their land. You know, if the energy company were *genuinely* interested in working alongside the islanders, then they would have come back with a modified proposal, along the lines of shared ownership'.

'But wind is a clean source of energy?' the reporter replied. 'Given the environmental safeguards which are in place for developments such as these, surely you must agree, that wind does in fact go a long way to reducing the carbon footprint, and the country's dependence upon fossil fuels?'

'The Government abandoned its planned environmental safeguards', John informed, which indeed it had done. 'If they were genuinely so interested in promoting green energy, they would maybe have looked at something like a solar farm for the island instead'.

Jean and Rhea had been watching the news report from Jean's house. She was aghast at the sight of her husband lying on the ground tied to a propeller with his arms outstretched.

'I better go and get him', she said to Rhea.

Both women left the house promptly and headed quickly along the Bria Main Road.

As the morning wore on, the other two policemen on the island arrived, alongwith a Special Constable. As they cleared the crowd that had formed at the entrance, the Sergeant opened the back of their van and took out a pair of garden shears.
Walking up to John, he tried again.

'Look, you've had your moment of fame and made your point, now release yourself and go home, or I will have to cut you both loose and arrest you'.

'I'll follow you to the end of the earth!' Archie shouted over again.

'Aye, and we'll stop at the Court on the way there!' the Policeman shouted back, beginning to lose patience.

'There is nothing in this world that will make me untie myself', said John. 'They will have to crucify me first'. He was resolute.

As the Police Sergeant stood there haggling with John, Jean appeared from the rear of the crowd.
On seeing her approach out the corner of his eye, the Sergeant turned aside to tell her that she 'must not come any closer, or you will end up being done for breach of the peace'.

'I've come to take him home', said Jean in a matter of fact manner, brushing past the Policeman and continuing on her path.

The Policeman stood aside, taken aback at just how brusque this small woman was with him. Jean went over and spoke quietly to her husband. Shortly thereafter, John released himself from the ropes, and walked over to Archie and undid the knots which bound him.

'It needed a woman's touch', smiled the big Policeman, and Jean and the two men walked away and down to the entrance which was clear, with the protesters standing, cheering, on both sides.

John expected to be arrested, but the big Sergeant was just pleased that the stand-off was over and no damage had been done, that he made no attempt to do so.

The two vans which had been full of workmen on the second site, and who had come outside and had sat patiently drinking tea from their flasks, eating sandwiches, while enjoying the entertainment at the top of the hill, now clambered back aboard the vans. They drove up the track and through the entrance to the first site.

The battle of Glen Bria was over.

THE FALL OUT

It was later that night at the pub, when all the day's events were recalled and retold a thousand times over, that Murdoch and Rhea asked Jean what she had done to make her husband release himself.

'Nothing much', she informed. 'I just told him he had won the moral high ground, but he could not win the war, and oh, that I had made some fudge for him which was back at the house'.

'Ah, the way to a man's heart is through his stomach', Rhea concluded.

Archie and John were the toast of the pub that night, and had absolutely no need to put their hands in their pockets, nor for many a month thereafter.

Calum was delighted at the business the campaign had generated for the pub, and for the following months over the holiday season.

Many of the events surrounding the campaign were recounted over the bar, largely for the benefit of the tourists who came for their summer holidays, and who wanted to know everything that had happened.

The exploits of Archie and John took on legendary status, and many of those who spent their vacation on the island, came to the pub in the hope of catching a glimpse of either one, or both, of them.

If that did not happen, Calum had put up one of the posters from the original march to the Council chamber. He had a badge (the original **F.A.R.T.** one), one of the ropes used to secure John to the Wind Turbine blades, the cartridge from the flare that was fired in the bay, and a copy of John's speech to the Council, put in a glass cabinet in the bar. People could view them there and somehow feel part of the campaign, by being so close to its history through the artefacts on display.

So, for the first year, the campaign had seemed like a needless, though entertaining, novelty to the visiting tourists.
But in time, the implications of the development started to impact island life. It has changed quite significantly over the last few years.

Bria village on the island is now mainly all holiday homes, with local people choosing to move off the island which they felt was becoming increasingly industrialised and visually blighted.

As a result, the secondary school on the island was no longer able to support fifth and sixth year education. Both the school roll and the number of teachers had declined. Now, the older pupils have to take the ferry each day and complete their higher education at the secondary school in the town on the mainland, where the ferry port is situated.

The local cottage hospital was no longer able to provide Accident and Emergency facilities, and patients who are required to attend the hospital, now have to travel to the mainland, which is quite some distance from the pier where the ferry berths.

Murdoch and Rhea also left to live on the mainland, albeit with a heavy heart. Murdoch needed more and more help with his disability, as he never regained his mobility. He also became dependent and needed increasing help with personal care, which he did not wish to burden his wife with.

Sadly, due to the migration of the islanders from their land, there were simply no longer the number of carers left on the island to undertake these tasks.

Similarly, Jeanette, the youngest daughter of John and Jean left the island, as the Care Home, which co-incidentally Murdoch could have had respite care in, had been forced to close on account of the same difficulty attracting staff.

Before he left, Murdoch poignantly noted that despite the promise of jobs, the new Wind Farm was operated remotely from the mainland.

Archie is still there, in the house nearest to the Shee Gate. However, quite a few of the crofters whose land lay on the far side of the Glen, which borders the new Wind Farm, finally gave up that way of life. The rough ground on the Glen, and the removal of the shielings, up where they would take their sheep and cattle to graze during the summer months, were now under the shadows of the giant propellers.

John goes over to Archie's for a drink every now and again.

Unfortunately, the hotel in which Calum ran his bar had been sold off, and now lies derelict. Far worse, as far as John is concerned, is that the shop which Mike ran, is now an off licence. It does not sell fudge.

In the village of Clachan, work has begun to demolish and build a new village hall, but there is now less of a demand for its facilities.

BRIA WOODS

These are the woods at Glen Bria, shortly after sunset, on a clear summer's night.

The hypnotic sound of swishing blades buffeting the air can be heard, tirelessly beating their rhythm, over and over again.

The wise old men who were once clad in ivy, are no longer there to impart their timeless wisdom to all who pass by them, in this ancient of Glens.

The horses are still in the nearby field, the field being visible from the track now, as some of the trees that had previously hidden them from view, have been removed.

The squirrels have left, joined by the buzzard, as have all the birds of prey. Either the relentless noise of the turbines, or their blades, made the Bria Woods a dangerous environment in which to make their homes.

The small lochan has now been joined by what used to be the larger puddle, due to a raised water table, and which is threatening to encroach on the large electric pylon situated beside it.

The only monoliths that are prominent now, are not the ones from ancient history, but instead are modern ones, comprising six enormous turbines with their rotating blades. When viewed from across the water on the mainland, they appear as dark spindles, silhouetted against a moonlit sky, casting their shadows on a dark island.

POSTFACE

The Deserted Village
by Oliver Goldsmith (1770)

Sweet Auburn, loveliest village of the plain,
Where health and plenty cheared the labouring swain,
Where smiling spring its earliest visit paid,
And parting summer's lingering blooms delayed,
Dear lovely bowers of innocence and ease,
Seats of my youth, when every sport could please,
How often have I loitered o'er thy green,
Where humble happiness endeared each scene!
How often have I paused on every charm,
The sheltered cot, the cultivated farm,
The never-failing brook, the busy mill,
The decent church that topt the neighbouring hill,

The hawthorn bush, with seats beneath the shade,

For talking age and whispering lovers made!

How often have I blest the coming day,

When toil remitting lent its turn to play,

And all the village train, from labour free,

Led up their sports beneath the spreading tree,

While many a pastime circled in the shade,

The young contending as the old surveyed;

And many a gambol frolicked o'er the ground,

And slights of art and feats of strength went round;

And still as each repeated pleasure tired,

Succeeding sports the mirthful band inspired;

The dancing pair that simply sought renown

By holding out to tire each other down;

The swain mistrustless of his smutted face,

While secret laughter tittered round the place;

The bashful virgin's side-long looks of love,

The matron's glance that would those looks reprove!
These were thy charms, sweet village; sports like these,
With sweet succession, taught even toil to please;
These round thy bowers their chearful influence shed,
These were thy charms—But all these charms are fled.
Sweet smiling village, loveliest of the lawn,
Thy sports are fled, and all thy charms withdrawn;
Amidst thy bowers the tyrant's hand is seen,
And desolation saddens all thy green:
One only master grasps the whole domain,
And half a tillage stints thy smiling plain;
No more thy glassy brook reflects the day,
But, choaked with sedges, works its weedy way;
Along thy glades, a solitary guest,

The hollow-sounding bittern guards its nest;

Amidst thy desert walks the lapwing flies,

And tires their echoes with unvaried cries.

Sunk are thy bowers, in shapeless ruin all,

And the long grass o'ertops the mouldering wall;

And, trembling, shrinking from the spoiler's hand,

Far, far away, thy children leave the land.

Ill fares the land, to hastening ills a prey,

Where wealth accumulates, and men decay:

Princes and lords may flourish, or may fade;

A breath can make them, as a breath has made;

But a bold peasantry, their country's pride,

When once destroyed, can never be supplied.

A time there was, ere England's griefs began,

When every rood of ground maintained its man;

For him light labour spread her wholesome store,

Just gave what life required, but gave no more:

His best companions, innocence and health;

And his best riches, ignorance of wealth.

But times are altered; trade's unfeeling train

Usurp the land and dispossess the swain;

Along the lawn, where scattered hamlets rose,

Unwieldy wealth and cumbrous pomp repose;

And every want to oppulence allied,

And every pang that folly pays to pride.

Those gentle hours that plenty bade to bloom,

Those calm desires that asked but little room,

Those healthful sports that graced the peaceful scene,

Lived in each look, and brightened all the green;

These, far departing seek a kinder shore,

And rural mirth and manners are no more.

Sweet Auburn! parent of the blissful hour,

Thy glades forlorn confess the tyrant's power.

Here as I take my solitary rounds,

Amidst thy tangling walks, and ruined grounds,
And, many a year elapsed, return to view
Where once the cottage stood, the hawthorn grew,
Remembrance wakes with all her busy train,
Swells at my breast, and turns the past to pain.
In all my wanderings round this world of care,
In all my griefs—and God has given my share—
I still had hopes, my latest hours to crown,
Amidst these humble bowers to lay me down;
To husband out life's taper at the close,
And keep the flame from wasting by repose.
I still had hopes, for pride attends us still,
Amidst the swains to shew my book-learned skill,
Around my fire an evening groupe to draw,
And tell of all I felt, and all I saw;
And, as an hare whom hounds and horns pursue,

Pants to the place from whence at first she flew,
I still had hopes, my long vexations past,
Here to return—and die at home at last.
O blest retirement, friend to life's decline,
Retreats from care that never must be mine,
How happy he who crowns, in shades like these
A youth of labour with an age of ease;
Who quits a world where strong temptations try,
And, since 'tis hard to combat, learns to fly!
For him no wretches, born to work and weep,
Explore the mine, or tempt the dangerous deep;
No surly porter stands in guilty state
To spurn imploring famine from the gate,
But on he moves to meet his latter end,
Angels around befriending virtue's friend;
Bends to the grave with unperceived decay,
While resignation gently slopes the way;
And, all his prospects brightening to the last,

His Heaven commences ere the world be past!
Sweet was the sound, when oft at evening's close,
Up yonder hill the village murmur rose;
There, as I past with careless steps and slow,
The mingling notes came soften'd from below;
The swain responsive as the milk-maid sung,
The sober herd that lowed to meet their young,
The noisy geese that gabbled o'er the pool,
The playful children just let loose from school,
The watch-dog's voice that bayed the whispering wind,
And the loud laugh that spoke the vacant mind,
These all in sweet confusion sought the shade,
And filled each pause the nightingale had made.
But now the sounds of population fail,
No cheerful murmurs fluctuate in the gale,
No busy steps the grass-grown foot-way tread,
For all the bloomy flush of life is fled.
All but yon widowed, solitary thing

That feebly bends beside the plashy spring;
She, wretched matron, forced in age, for bread,
To strip the brook with mantling cresses spread,
To pick her wintry faggot from the thorn,
To seek her nightly shed, and weep till morn;
She only left of all the harmless train,
The sad historian of the pensive plain.
Near yonder copse, where once the garden smiled,
And still where many a garden-flower grows wild;
There, where a few torn shrubs the place disclose,
The village preacher's modest mansion rose.
A man he was, to all the country dear,
And passing rich with forty pounds a year;
Remote from towns he ran his godly race,
Nor e'er had changed, nor wished to change his place;

Unpractised he to fawn, or seek for power,
By doctrines fashioned to the varying hour;
Far other aims his heart had learned to prize,
More skilled to raise the wretched than to rise.
His house was known to all the vagrant train,
He chid their wanderings but relieved their pain;
The long-remembered beggar was his guest,
Whose beard descending swept his aged breast;
The ruined spendthrift, now no longer proud,
Claim'd kindred there, and had his claims allowed;
The broken soldier, kindly bade to stay,
Sate by his fire, and talked the night away;
Wept o'er his wounds, or, tales of sorrow done,
Shouldered his crutch, and shewed how fields were won.
Pleased with his guests, the good man learned to glow,
And quite forgot their vices in their woe;

Careless their merits, or their faults to scan,
His pity gave ere charity began.
Thus to relieve the wretched was his pride,
And even his failings leaned to Virtue's side;
But in his duty prompt at every call,
He watched and wept, he prayed and felt, for all.
And, as a bird each fond endearment tries,
To tempt its new-fledged offspring to the skies;
He tried each art, reproved each dull delay,
Allured to brighter worlds, and led the way.
Beside the bed where parting life was layed,
And sorrow, guilt, and pain, by turns, dismayed
The reverend champion stood. At his control
Despair and anguish fled the struggling soul;
Comfort came down the trembling wretch to raise,
And his last faltering accents whispered praise.
At church, with meek and unaffected grace,
His looks adorned the venerable place;

Truth from his lips prevailed with double sway,
And fools, who came to scoff, remained to pray.
The service past, around the pious man,
With steady zeal, each honest rustic ran;
Even children followed, with endearing wile,
And plucked his gown, to share the good man's smile.
His ready smile a parent's warmth exprest,
Their welfare pleased him, and their cares distrest:
To them his heart, his love, his griefs were given,
But all his serious thoughts had rest in Heaven.
As some tall cliff that lifts its awful form,
Swells from the vale, and midway leaves the storm,
Tho' round its breast the rolling clouds are spread,
Eternal sunshine settles on its head.

Beside yon straggling fence that skirts the way,
With blossomed furze unprofitably gay,
There, in his noisy mansion, skill'd to rule,
The village master taught his little school;
A man severe he was, and stern to view,
I knew him well, and every truant knew;
Well had the boding tremblers learned to trace
The day's disasters in his morning face;
Full well they laughed, with counterfeited glee,
At all his jokes, for many a joke had he:
Full well the busy whisper circling round,
Conveyed the dismal tidings when he frowned;
Yet he was kind, or if severe in aught,
The love he bore to learning was in fault;
The village all declared how much he knew;
'Twas certain he could write, and cypher too;
Lands he could measure, terms and tides presage,
And ev'n the story ran that he could gauge.
In arguing too, the parson owned his skill,

For even tho' vanquished, he could argue still;
While words of learned length and thundering sound,
Amazed the gazing rustics ranged around;
And still they gazed, and still the wonder grew,
That one small head could carry all he knew.
But past is all his fame. The very spot
Where many a time he triumphed, is forgot.
Near yonder thorn, that lifts its head on high,
Where once the sign-post caught the passing eye,
Low lies that house where nut-brown draughts inspired,
Where grey-beard mirth and smiling toil retired,
Where village statesmen talked with looks profound,
And news much older than their ale went round.
Imagination fondly stoops to trace
The parlour splendours of that festive place;

The white-washed wall, the nicely sanded floor,
The varnished clock that clicked behind the door;
The chest contrived a double debt to pay,
A bed by night, a chest of drawers by day;
The pictures placed for ornament and use,
The twelve good rules, the royal game of goose;
The hearth, except when winter chill'd the day,
With aspen boughs, and flowers, and fennel gay;
While broken tea-cups, wisely kept for shew,
Ranged o'er the chimney, glistened in a row.
Vain transitory splendours! Could not all
Reprieve the tottering mansion from its fall!
Obscure it sinks, nor shall it more impart
An hour's importance to the poor man's heart;
Thither no more the peasant shall repair
To sweet oblivion of his daily care;
No more the farmer's news, the barber's tale,
No more the woodman's ballad shall prevail;

No more the smith his dusky brow shall clear,
Relax his ponderous strength, and lean to hear;
The host himself no longer shall be found
Careful to see the mantling bliss go round;
Nor the coy maid, half willing to be prest,
Shall kiss the cup to pass it to the rest.
Yes! let the rich deride, the proud disdain,
These simple blessings of the lowly train;
To me more dear, congenial to my heart,
One native charm, than all the gloss of art;
Spontaneous joys, where Nature has its play,
The soul adopts, and owns their first-born sway;
Lightly they frolic o'er the vacant mind,
Unenvied, unmolested, unconfined.
But the long pomp, the midnight masquerade,
With all the freaks of wanton wealth arrayed,
In these, ere triflers half their wish obtain,
The toiling pleasure sickens into pain;
And, even while fashion's brightest arts decoy,

The heart distrusting asks, if this be joy.
Ye friends to truth, ye statesmen who survey
The rich man's joys encrease, the poor's decay,
'Tis yours to judge, how wide the limits stand
Between a splendid and a happy land.
Proud swells the tide with loads of freighted ore,
And shouting Folly hails them from her shore;
Hoards even beyond the miser's wish abound,
And rich men flock from all the world around.
Yet count our gains. This wealth is but a name
That leaves our useful products still the same.
Not so the loss. The man of wealth and pride
Takes up a space that many poor supplied;
Space for his lake, his park's extended bounds,
Space for his horses, equipage, and hounds:
The robe that wraps his limbs in silken sloth,
Has robbed the neighbouring fields of half their growth;
His seat, where solitary sports are seen,

Indignant spurns the cottage from the green:
Around the world each needful product flies,
For all the luxuries the world supplies.
While thus the land adorned for pleasure, all
In barren splendour feebly waits the fall.
As some fair female unadorned and plain,
Secure to please while youth confirms her reign,
Slights every borrowed charm that dress supplies,
Nor shares with art the triumph of her eyes.
But when those charms are past, for charms are frail,
When time advances, and when lovers fail,
She then shines forth, solicitous to bless,
In all the glaring impotence of dress.
Thus fares the land, by luxury betrayed:
In nature's simplest charms at first arrayed;
But verging to decline, its splendours rise,
Its vistas strike, its palaces surprize;

While, scourged by famine from the smiling land,
The mournful peasant leads his humble band;
And while he sinks, without one arm to save,
The country blooms—a garden, and a grave.
Where then, ah where, shall poverty reside,
To scape the pressure of contiguous pride?
If to some common's fenceless limits strayed,
He drives his flock to pick the scanty blade,
Those fenceless fields the sons of wealth divide,
And ev'n the bare-worn common is denied.
If to the city sped—What waits him there?
To see profusion that he must not share;
To see ten thousand baneful arts combined
To pamper luxury, and thin mankind;
To see those joys the sons of pleasure know,
Extorted from his fellow-creature's woe.
Here while the courtier glitters in brocade,
There the pale artist plies the sickly trade;

Here while the proud their long-drawn pomps display,
There the black gibbet glooms beside the way.
The dome where Pleasure holds her midnight reign,
Here, richly deckt, admits the gorgeous train;
Tumultuous grandeur crowds the blazing square,
The rattling chariots clash, the torches glare.
Sure scenes like these no troubles e'er annoy!
Sure these denote one universal joy!
Are these thy serious thoughts?—Ah, turn thine eyes
Where the poor houseless shivering female lies.
She once, perhaps, in village plenty blest,
Has wept at tales of innocence distrest;
Her modest looks the cottage might adorn
Sweet as the primrose peeps beneath the thorn:
Now lost to all; her friends, her virtue fled,
Near her betrayer's door she lays her head,

And, pinch'd with cold, and shrinking from the shower,
With heavy heart deplores that luckless hour
When idly first, ambitious of the town,
She left her wheel and robes of country brown.
Do thine, sweet Auburn, thine, the loveliest train,
Do thy fair tribes participate her pain?
Even now, perhaps, by cold and hunger led,
At proud men's doors they ask a little bread!
Ah, no. To distant climes, a dreary scene,
Where half the convex world intrudes between,
Through torrid tracts with fainting steps they go,
Where wild Altama murmurs to their woe.
Far different there from all that charm'd before,
The various terrors of that horrid shore;
Those blazing suns that dart a downward ray,
And fiercely shed intolerable day;
Those matted woods where birds forget to sing,

But silent bats in drowsy clusters cling;
Those poisonous fields with rank luxuriance crowned,
Where the dark scorpion gathers death around;
Where at each step the stranger fears to wake
The rattling terrors of the vengeful snake;
Where crouching tigers wait their hapless prey,
And savage men, more murderous still than they;
While oft in whirls the mad tornado flies,
Mingling the ravaged landscape with the skies.
Far different these from every former scene,
The cooling brook, the grassy vested green,
The breezy covert of the warbling grove,
That only shelter'd thefts of harmless love.
Good Heaven! what sorrows gloom'd that parting day,
That called them from their native walks away;
When the poor exiles, every pleasure past,

Hung round their bowers, and fondly looked their last,
And took a long farewell, and wished in vain
For seats like these beyond the western main;
And shuddering still to face the distant deep,
Returned and wept, and still returned to weep.
The good old sire the first prepared to go
To new found worlds, and wept for others woe.
But for himself, in conscious virtue brave,
He only wished for worlds beyond the grave.
His lovely daughter, lovelier in her tears,
The fond companion of his helpless years,
Silent went next, neglectful of her charms,
And left a lover's for a father's arms.
With louder plaints the mother spoke her woes,
And blessed the cot where every pleasure rose;
And kist her thoughtless babes with many a tear,
And claspt them close, in sorrow doubly dear;
Whilst her fond husband strove to lend relief

In all the silent manliness of grief.
O luxury! thou curst by Heaven's decree,
How ill exchanged are things like these for thee!
How do thy potions, with insidious joy,
Diffuse their pleasures only to destroy!
Kingdoms, by thee, to sickly greatness grown,
Boast of a florid vigour not their own;
At every draught more large and large they grow,
A bloated mass of rank unwieldy woe;
Till sapped their strength, and every part unsound,
Down, down they sink, and spread a ruin round.
Even now the devastation is begun,
And half the business of destruction done;
Even now, methinks, as pondering here I stand,
I see the rural virtues leave the land:
Down where yon anchoring vessel spreads the sail,

That idly waiting flaps with every gale,
Downward they move, a melancholy band,
Pass from the shore, and darken all the strand.
Contented toil, and hospitable care,
And kind connubial tenderness, are there;
And piety with wishes placed above,
And steady loyalty, and faithful love.
And thou, sweet Poetry, thou loveliest maid,
Still first to fly where sensual joys invade;
Unfit in these degenerate times of shame,
To catch the heart, or strike for honest fame;
Dear charming nymph, neglected and decried,
My shame in crowds, my solitary pride;
Thou source of all my bliss, and all my woe,
That found'st me poor at first, and keep'st me so;
Thou guide by which the nobler arts excell,
Thou nurse of every virtue, fare thee well!
Farewell, and O where'er thy voice be tried,
On Torno's cliffs, or Pambamarca's side,

Whether were equinoctial fervours glow,
Or winter wraps the polar world in snow,
Still let thy voice, prevailing over time,
Redress the rigours of the inclement clime;
Aid slighted truth with thy persuasive strain,
Teach erring man to spurn the rage of gain;
Teach him, that states of native strength possest,
Tho' very poor, may still be very blest;
That trade's proud empire hastes to swift decay,
As ocean sweeps the labour'd mole away;
While self-dependent power can time defy,
As rocks resist the billows and the sky.

Printed in Dunstable, United Kingdom